RUNNING

PAM BLOOM

Running

Published by Pam Bloom Publishing

ISBN: 978-0-9955272-3-2

Cover design by Ilan Sheady,
www.ilanimationstudios.com

Author's note: This book was written and produced in the UK, and uses British English language conventions.

Also by Pam Bloom: Whole New World[s],
Book 1 in The Parallel Universe Adventures.

For my daughter, Annabel.

Read it one day; you'll enjoy it!

Connect with the author at

www.pambloomauthor.com

Sign up for Pam's email list

and you will be sent FREE scifi reads

Don't miss out!

The alarm

We'd been settled – happy, content, normal – for only around five months when it all changed. When *they* came. When we had to start running.

It was the middle of a cold February night, and I remember I was deep in a dream about my other reality brother, Ivan – he was flying above me, smiling, in an angel-type way – when a persistent beeping dragged me up from dreamland and back to reality – my reality, at least.

BEEP... BEEP... BEEP... it went. Ivan flew away, my head started to hurt, and I opened my eyes quickly. Smoke alarm? Was the house on fire? Quick, I had to get Lizzie and mum out of the house before we were all overcome with smoke.

I threw back the covers and got out of bed, in the process nearly treading on my best friend Jake, who in my dreamlike haze I'd forgotten was sleeping over – it was half term holidays and he was lying on a blow-up bed next to mine. I stood on his leg in my haste to get to the door. “OUCH!” he protested.

“You awake, then?” I asked him.

“Yes, fool,” he said, kind as ever. Jake’s a great mate, and very intelligent, but not very tactful. Or practical, either. He was trying to scramble out of his sleeping bag. I leant down and helped him by undoing the zip a little.

BEEP... BEEP... went the noise.

“Quick!” I said. “It must be the smoke alarm. We have to tell the others.”

Jake mumbled something about it not sounding like the smoke alarm, and there not being any smoke to smell, but followed me anyway out of the bedroom door and onto the landing.

I was heading to Lizzie’s room when her door opened and she came out, looking confused. “What is it Ethan?” she said, hurrying towards me. Dressed in her spotty yellow pyjamas and clutching her beloved, ragged teddy bear she looked younger than her eight years. Not just young but frightened, and my first instinct as her big brother, as always, was to protect her.

I put an arm round her, said: “It doesn’t sound like the smoke alarm – maybe it’s just run out of batteries or something.” Then I turned quickly to mum’s bedroom, and was about to knock on the door when Samuel opened it. His greying long hair was uncombed but he was fully dressed in jeans, sweatshirt and walking boots – which I thought a little odd, seeing it was obviously the middle of the night.

Samuel – or Sam, to his friends – is mum’s boyfriend. He moved in last September after a little adventure we had in the summer, and has been part of the family since then.

I should explain that Samuel was not born in our reality, but in a parallel, or alternate, one. An agent for the Institute of Alternative Reality Technology (or I-ART for short), he arrived in our lives after I found – and accidentally used – his device for travelling from one reality to another. These DARTs (Devices for Alternative Reality Transportation) are small, pebble-like things that can take you to any of millions of parallel worlds at the touch of a button.

Faced with redundancy when his agency went bust, Sam had arrived in our reality by mistake, but could not return to his own because he would be arrested for running away – and maybe put on trial for desertion.

Last time I'd seen him, the night before, he had been telling us all over dinner about a hilarious adventure he'd had some years ago when he DARTed to a reality in which dinosaurs had never been made extinct. We'd all laughed until tears were running down our faces.

He was not looking amused now. In fact, he looked frightened, which scared me more than anything, because I'd never seen him like that before. Angry, yes, but more usually cool, in control. Something was obviously not right.

BEEP... BEEP... BEEP... went the alarm.

Samuel shouted above its noise. He sounded upset.

"Everyone go and get dressed. For outside. Shoes

and all. The house is not on fire, but you need to get dressed as quickly as you can, then come downstairs." We all looked blankly at him. "NOW!" he shouted.

Something in his voice told us he meant business. We all turned and went back into our rooms, quickly found clothes and climbed into them. As we were doing so, thankfully, the beeping stopped. Jake and I continued in silence, confused, dreading what this could mean.

Both of us had first-hand experience of dangerous situations, having travelled to a different reality last summer to try to stop my 'dad' in that reality from bullying his children – an alternative Lizzie and my other reality 'brother' Ivan. Despite our good intentions it had not ended well, resulting in Ivan getting shot and us nearly being trapped forever with no way of getting home. Only Sam's timely arrival had saved us. So we trusted him with our lives.

Dressed for outdoors, we came back out to find Lizzie standing, bewildered, on the landing. I was glad to see she had put jeans and a jumper on, not one of her girly dresses. She, too, knew that Samuel wouldn't tell us to do something like this if it wasn't serious, and she looked terrified.

I grabbed her hand – the one that wasn't still clutching the teddy – and led her downstairs. Jake followed.

When we got down to the hall I was astonished to see the front door was open and Sam was busy loading the car up with rucksacks. I tried to ask him what was going on, but he just gestured down the hall and went out of the door with another load.

In the kitchen mum was sitting on a chair, looking strained. She, too, was fully dressed, in warm clothing, although her hair was untidy. She was pulling at it in the manner of someone waiting for bad news.

When we entered she told us all to sit down. We did so, Lizzie sitting on mum's knee, and I glanced at the clock. It was half past three. The heating wasn't on, of course, and it was freezing. We were all shivering, and I don't expect it was purely because of the cold.

“Mum, what’s...?” was as far as I got, before she shut me up with a: “Sam will explain. I have to help him.”

And with that she picked Lizzie up and put her on her own chair, despite her protesting, and went out of the room.

“Well, that was informative,” said Jake wryly. The three of us sat there, waiting, for around five minutes, before mum and Sam returned. Mum stood by the door, biting her nails, while Sam sat down in the chair she had recently left. He still looked scared.

Before we could say a word, he held up his hand to silence us. “We don't have time for questions,” he said. His voice was serious but calm, and I knew he had regained control of the situation, whatever it was.

He looked at us all in turn, sitting in front of him, people from another reality he’d come to care about very deeply, and said: “That beeping was not the smoke alarm. It was a warning alarm I set up not long after I got here to tell us when someone was transporting into this reality. I can’t tell who it is – or even from what reality they're coming – but it means someone is on their way. And whoever it is, they're probably not coming just to say hello."

We all stared at him. He went on, sad now: "I'm so, so sorry to have dragged you into my world. But I can't leave you here – there's no telling what they'd do to find me. I have to keep you all safe." He looked up at mum, who gave him a tired and thin smile, then added: "We have to go. Now."

And he got up from the table and started ushering us out of the door like sheep.

"Your coats, some clothes and most precious belongings are already in the car," he said, putting an arm round Lizzie to show her the way out. "Everything else can be left behind. You can sleep on the way."

Mum got hold of Lizzie's hand and guided her to the front door. "But where are we going?" she asked, not unreasonably, I thought.

Mum looked at Sam. "Somewhere safer than here," was all he'd say.

And so it was that three tired, upset and bewildered children were bundled into Sam's Jeep – he'd bought it just three months ago after getting a job as a countryside ranger – along with all the rucksacks and bags, some of which, I saw, were full of tinned food. We might be a while, then, I thought.

Sam and mum got in the front, told us all to belt up, and Sam reversed out of the driveway. As he did, I looked up at our house and wondered if we'd ever see it again.

I didn't know it then, thankfully, but it would be quite a while before we did.

The barn

Soon Lizzie and Jake had dozed off, Lizzie in the middle, her head lolling onto my shoulder, mouth open and dribbling slightly onto my jumper. I didn't mind – let her sleep.

I shut my eyes but couldn't manage to join her, despite the time. There was a bag digging into my left leg – from the feel of it, it had tins of food in it – but that wasn't what was keeping me awake; not really. It was the total dread at what Sam had said back in the house.

If someone was DARTing into our reality, it wouldn't be just a coincidence. They had to be coming for Sam. And if they were coming for Sam, we were all in danger.

After a while we reached the motorway and started heading south. I wondered idly where we were going, if Sam knew or was just driving in a random direction. Knowing him, he'd have a plan.

The monotony of the motorway, especially in the dark, with the lights whizzing past at regular intervals, soon sent me off to sleep, but I woke an hour or so later, cramped, confused and disorientated, to the sound of mum and Sam talking in low voices. Pretending to still be asleep, I listened to their conversation.

"...have to be there for some time?" mum was asking.

"I don't know, Heather," Sam said wearily. "I hope not."

"But what about Jake? We can't just kidnap him – his parents will be expecting him back tomorrow evening. They'll ring the police if he just disappears."

I'd thought of this, too. It was all very well going on the run with your own flesh and blood, but taking a friend along as well was not advisable. Sam seemed to have thought of this.

He said: "I'll ring his parents and tell them he's staying with us until the weekend. That'll buy us a few days, at least. They might object, but I think I can persuade them."

Being a former agent, Sam had many tricks up his sleeve, including the ability to talk his way out of tricky situations. I was sure he'd be able to sweet-talk Jake's parents with some lie or other.

"But still," mum was saying, "shouldn't we just drop him off at home? He'll be safe there – they won't be after *him*, will they?"

Sam looked over at her and frowned. He paused, and a chill went down my spine.

"I honestly don't know," he said, slowly. "I told you before everyone who travels between realities can be traced because they collect radiation. They – whoever they are – will undoubtedly be able to find him if they want to. I'm not taking that chance."

There was silence for a couple of seconds, just the engine's noise to hear, then he went on: "I care for you all too much to let you fall into the hands of anyone who may be after me."

Mum was quiet after this, and the engine noise soon sent me back to sleep, where I had horrible dreams about Jake, glowing green from radiation, running in front of me along a dark pathway.

Try as hard as I could, I just couldn't quite reach him.

....

I woke once more when the car stopped. I opened my eyes and saw mum and Sam both getting out. It was that half-light you get near dawn, and I guessed a couple of hours had passed, at least, since I'd gone to sleep. I was stiff as a board, and had no idea where we were.

Next to me Lizzie was still snoring, although she'd moved and now had her head on Jake's shoulder, her teddy clutched to her chest. Jake was awake, too

"Where are we?" he asked with a yawn.

"I have no idea," I said, "but I'm going to find out." And I opened the door and got out, wincing at the cramps in my legs and back. Outside was freezing, and there was a cold wind blowing straight at me. I reached back into the car and got my coat from the back shelf, put it on then stood, looking around.

It was so dark. There were no street lights, and I couldn't see anything except a few trees to my left and, directly in front, a large barn-like building with a rickety double wooden door. It was ajar, and I guessed mum and Sam had gone inside. There was no other sign of life.

It was obviously not a five-star hotel.

I heard the car door shut, and Jake appeared, zipping his coat up and stamping his feet. "Jeez, it's cold," he said, rubbing his hands together. He looked at the building in front of us and curled his lip. "I hope they have electricity," he said.

"I doubt it," I mumbled, and started walking towards the door. Jake stopped me. "We can't leave Lizzie," he said. I looked back through the car window, and was just about to say she'd be OK when Sam came out of the door and told us to get inside out of the cold. We didn't need asking twice.

Inside was dark except for a pool of light in one corner. The first thing that hit you as you walked in was a sweet musty smell, but I couldn't make anything out. The hard, stone floor seemed to be covered with remnants of straw.

Not knowing what else to do, Jake and I slowly walked over towards the lit corner, and as we drew near I realised the source of the light was mum, lighting candles which she'd placed on a shelf. She had a small bag of tealights in one hand, and a box of matches in the other. As we approached she said to us: "Make yourselves useful – take some of these and put them on the boxes over there." She pointed to a pile of wooden crates to her left. They were neatly arranged in piles, mostly to waist height.

Jake and I took a few candles each and put them in clusters on the boxes. Then mum came over and lit them with the matches, a sulphury smell mingling with the sweetness of the air.

"That's better," she said. "It's beginning to look like home already."

I wasn't sure about that, but I think she was just trying to be cheerful for our sakes.

"Go and help Sam bring the stuff in out of the car," she said, and we walked over the stone floor again towards the door, though it was hard to see where it was.

On our way out we met Sam, on his way back in with an armful of bags. "Just bring everything in," he said, adding: "Leave Lizzie asleep for now; we'll bring her in last."

So Jake, Sam and I unloaded the car, piling everything into the corner near mum, who started sorting things into orderly piles. By the time we'd finished she had made a small area of the barn look quite homely, with sleeping bags placed on top of a straw base to keep us warm, food on top of a box and other stuff – plates, cups, pans, etc – on top of another. The candles cast a soft glow.

Last thing to be brought in was Lizzie, carried in Sam's arms like a baby, still groggy but awake. He put her down gently on top of a sleeping bag next to mum, who patted her hair. Jake and I sat next to her on our own sleeping bags.

Then Sam went outside again – “to hide the car” he said – and we were left alone in the semi-dark.

“Just where are we?” I asked mum, who was busying herself emptying a camping stove and utensils out of another bag.

She looked over at me and shrugged. “I’m not too sure,” she said. “Somewhere near Oxford, I think.” So at least three hours’ drive from home, I reckoned. She went on: “Sam found this barn a while ago – I think he knew this day would come, and wanted to find a safe place to hide out when it did.” She paused, then added: “I don’t think he thought it would be so soon, though.”

We sat there, tired, disorientated and not really knowing what to do, while mum tried to make the place orderly. Why do mums do that, I wondered? Wherever you are – at home, on a picnic, in a tent on holiday – mums always sort stuff out into orderly piles. I suppose it’s the motherly instinct to make a nest.

She was trying to find some cups so we could all

have a cup of tea – of course, everything looks better after a cup of tea – when Sam returned. It was getting light, and as I turned to watch him come in I noticed we really were in a barn, but it had obviously been empty for some time.

There were still beams on the ceiling, and a few low dividing walls along the far side, which contained odds and ends of old machinery and farm equipment. The floor was covered in a light dusting of straw, and there was a huge pile of old sacks in one corner. The double door was the only way in or out, and there were several small windows, a couple smashed, above head height. The thin light was just beginning to seep in through them. It certainly wasn't the Hilton, and I wondered how long we would have to stay there.

Sam helped mum set up the camping stove on the floor a little way away from our 'cosy corner,' then walked over to the opposite side of the barn and pulled back a dusty tarpaulin to reveal a store of bottled water – you know the biggest water bottles you can get? There were about ten of them. So Sam had prepared for this, then, I thought.

He dragged one of the bottles over to us now, opened it and poured some of it into a pan for boiling. "I hope you're not in a rush for a cup of tea, kids," he said – yeah, I'd been camping before, I knew it took ages for a pan of water to boil.

Just then Lizzie spoke up. She was obviously fully awake now, and not in the least bit happy with the present situation. "I want to go home!" she wailed, in a petulant little kid voice she usually reserved for when she was sent to bed.

Mum sighed and pulled her onto her knee, cradling her with one arm while the other put tea bags into cups. "We can't, honey," she said. "We've only just got here."

"But why are we here?" Lizzie asked, voicing what all of us were probably thinking.

Sam pulled a wooden box down from a pile and sat on it. It looked like those old tea chests you used to get; sturdy enough to sit on, anyway.

Mum was looking at Sam expectantly. He sighed, then said: “I told you we had to run away from whoever it is who’s DARTing into this reality. Removing ourselves from the house buys us time, because they can’t follow us quickly if we don’t use the DART. They won’t know where we’ve gone; not for a while, anyway. So we’re safe for now.”

He was about to go on, but Jake, who had been very quiet for him, interrupted. “How long are we safe for?” he asked.

We all looked at Sam, who shrugged. “If we don’t use the DARTs, maybe a few weeks...”

“A few weeks!” said Jake, shocked. “You mean we have to stay here for that long?”

“...but not forever, because they can trace our signal,” Sam went on. “You remember, boys, how I traced my DART to your house when Ethan picked it up?” We nodded. “Well, they’ll be able to trace the DARTs in our possession, though they won’t want to stay in this reality to do it – and it’s harder if you’re elsewhere. It really depends who they are and what they want, but in a week or two we'll have to think about moving on again."

Great, I thought. It looked like we were going to spend the next few weeks in a cold, draughty barn – and then the rest of our lives on the run.

Waiting

In the end it felt like weeks, but actually it was only five days we spent in that draughty old barn. On reflection, they weren't *bad* days – I've since had much worse, as you'll find out.

Sure, it was cold, though we soon put most of our clothes on and spent much of our time snuggled up in sleeping bags and blankets. It was also smelly, and I'm pretty sure there were rats at night, though we never actually saw one.

We didn't go hungry – Sam had got lots of food together just in case, and mum spent most of her time preparing three meals a day out of tins and packets. Some of it was really nice, too.

The main problem was boredom. Sam insisted we weren't allowed out of the barn at all unless it was to go to the toilet – I use the word toilet loosely, as actually we had to go in the bushes outside. This, as you can imagine, wasn't at all pleasant, especially at night, so we kept those visits as short as possible.

The barn was big enough to run around in, if we wanted exercise, and mum kept us busy washing pans, keeping our corner tidy, and playing card games. Sam had brought plenty of paper, pens and crayons for Lizzie, and several books for us to read, so we did have enough to do, although we complained like anything about being cooped up all day. And Lizzie never shut up about missing the TV. It was like being stuck in a caravan on a wet week away, only without the little shop to visit.

On the fourth afternoon me and Lizzie were arguing over something and Jake was lying on his sleeping bag, trying to read, when Sam suddenly stood up from his box seat, where he seemed to spend most of his time thinking.

"Right," he announced to the room in general. Lizzie and I went on squabbling, so he raised his voice. "Right!" he repeated. We stopped what we were doing and looked at him.

"Left!" mumbled Jake from behind his book.

Sam turned to him. “What?” he said, impatiently, flicking his long fringe out of his eyes.

Jake looked up. “Left!” he said. Sam stared at him. Jake went on: “I thought it was a word association game. Sorry. Do go on.”

Sam sat down again. “I’ve come to a decision,” he said, ignoring Jake.

Mum came over from the far corner, where she’d been tidying the water bottles for the third time that day. I think she, too, was bored out of her skull. She sat down on a box opposite Sam.

Sam looked at her, and I could see tears in his eyes. This wasn’t going to be an announcement we could all go home, then, I thought.

“What is it, dear?” mum asked, gently.

Sam shut his eyes for a second, then said: “We can’t live like this forever. Apart from the fact the kids have got to go back to school...” Lizzie groaned “...and Jake has to go home before his parents call the police, which will, I fear, be pretty soon from what they’ve been saying on the phone...” Jake tutted

"...we're all going to end up killing each other if we have to stay in hiding for much longer."

"Hear, hear," I said, staring pointedly at my sister. Sam stopped. "So what's the plan?" asked mum.

Sam sighed, a big, long sigh. "I have to leave," he said.

"Leave?" Jake, mum and I all said together.

Sam smiled. "Not forever," he said. Mum sighed with relief. Despite everything – having to hide in this stinky barn, not knowing when, if ever, we'd go home again – we all knew we didn't want Sam to leave us. He meant too much to us now.

He went on: "I mean I have to go home – back to my reality, that is – to find out what's going on. I've got friends, former colleagues, there who I can call on for help; insiders from I-ART, who should be able to tell me who it is that's looking for me – and why."

"But that's too dangerous; you said so yourself," said mum. "If you DART home they'll be able to trace you."

"I know, honey," said Sam, "but we can't go on

like this. If it was just me, I'd be happy running and living rough until the day I die – well, maybe not happy, but you get my meaning. But I've dragged all of you into this mess, and I have to get you out of it. The only way is to find out who's after me, and what they want. Then maybe I can find a way to stop them."

Jake had put his book down and was sitting up. "But Sam, it might not be your Institute that's coming for you. It could be Duncan's," he said now.

Duncan was Sam's alternative reality 'brother' – a different version of him, if you like, from another reality – who we had encountered last summer. A sworn enemy of our friend, he too was an agent and had swapped his DART for one of Sam's. We believed Duncan's version of I-ART would be glad to get their DART back, too.

Sam nodded. "I know," he said, "and if I discover my lot have all taken early retirement and aren't interested in me anymore, I can tackle it a different way. But know your enemy is the first rule of battle."

Despite mum's protests, Sam insisted on leaving that afternoon to drive to London, where, in his reality, his closest friend lived. His plan was to DART when he got there, pay a swift visit to his friend, and find out all he could about the Institute's current status. If all went to plan, and he wasn't caught, he'd be back with us by morning.

We all hugged him tightly before he left. I was scared he'd never come back – and then what would we do? – but he kept assuring us he knew what he was doing. "I just have to be quick, that's all," he said. "The less time I'm there the less signal they have to trace me with. I'll be there and back quicker than a lightning strike."

We watched him go with heavy hearts, and spent the rest of the day anxious and miserable. Jake kept trying to read, Lizzie didn't stop crying and mum kept snapping at us all over nothing.

It was a relief when the light faded and we had to try to go to sleep, though that proved difficult. It was particularly cold that night, I remember, and even fully clothed I was freezing under my thick sleeping bag and several blankets. I woke several times during the night, every time hoping Sam had woken me by coming back, but when morning came, drizzly and miserable, he still had not returned.

We were all silent, worried sick that something had happened to him. Mum looked like she hadn't slept all night, which I suspect was true, and the rest of us weren't much better.

We busied ourselves making breakfast. Mum insisted on using up the last of the bacon and sausages before they went mouldy, although none of us wanted to eat anything. We were sitting around, picking at our food, when suddenly the double doors burst open and Sam rushed in.

Thank goodness! We all stood up, mum rushed to hug him, and everyone started talking at once.

"Were you seen?" asked Jake. "Did you find out what's happening?" I asked. "Are you OK?" was mum's question. Lizzie, typically, asked if he had brought her any sweets.

Sam looked dishevelled and exhausted, and shushed us all as he shut the doors behind him and came to sit by the camping stove, which was our only source of heat so was kept on most of the time.

Mum quickly went to put a pan of water on to make him a cup of tea, while we all sat round in a circle, waiting for him to speak. It felt like storytime at primary school, when you all sit on the mat and the teacher reads you a book. Only this, of course, was not as much fun.

"Thank goodness you're all OK," was his first sentence, and I wondered why he was concerned about us when it was he who'd been in danger. I soon found out.

"Come and sit down, Heather," he said to mum, "I need to tell you what's going on."

Mum left the pan heating up and joined us on the sleeping bags on the floor, putting an arm around Lizzie for comfort.

"Well?" she said, "what's happening?"

Sam looked at us all, his new family, sitting in

front of him, and began: “It’s worse than I thought. We’re all in danger, here and anywhere we go. And it’s all my fault.”

Bad news

Sam had driven to London the previous afternoon with no trouble. He'd kept stopping to make sure he wasn't being followed, but had made good time and reached the city in the evening.

Parking in a multi-storey car park on the edge of the city, he'd left the car and travelled some way by underground, wanting to get as close as he could to his friend's house before he DARTed back to his reality.

"He lives on the second floor of a terraced house in the suburbs of our London, which is very like your own," he explained. "We even have the same underground system, though there are some differences."

He reached his destination with no problems and DARTed in the middle of a park, behind a bush, making sure no-one was around first. Confident he had not been followed, he arrived in his reality and went straight to a phone box to ring his friend's mobile.

Apparently our money is different to theirs, so he had to 'reverse the charges' – that is, he got his friend to pay for the call.

"Damien and I have this arrangement," said Sam, "that I can ring him anytime and he'll come to an agreed rendezvous point as soon as he's able to get there. All I have to do is ring him and use a coded message to say I need his help."

At this point Jake interrupted him. "He's a good friend, then," he said.

Sam smiled grimly. "Well," he said, "it's more that he owes me a favour. I saved his life once, and he has yet to pay me back."

"Oh, do tell that story," said Lizzie eagerly. Young as she was, this was all a big adventure for her, and she had forgotten, for the moment at least, that we were apparently in danger.

Sam reached out from his perch on the box and patted her head. "Later, Lizzie, later," he said. "I have to finish this one first." Lizzie sat back, disappointed.

Sam went on: "So I rang Damien – thankfully he

answered his phone – and gave him the coded message. I hung up the phone and went across town to the meeting place – a park around two miles from Damien's home. I only had to wait ten minutes for him to turn up – he has a car. I got in the passenger seat and he drove off – it's safer to talk when you're driving, as you can see if anyone's following you."

"And what did he tell you?" I asked. My patience was thin, and I needed to find out what danger we were in.

Sam sighed. "Damien used to be an agent, like me, but left a couple of years ago. He still has contacts in I-ART and beyond – in the government and police – who he gets all the gossip from. So he knows what's going on.

"He knew I'd be in touch sooner or later, because he heard I'd deserted my position when they disbanded the agency, and the Institute would be after me. Of course they didn't know where I'd gone until I went back there last year..." (Sam had returned to his reality in the summer to obtain a false identity so he could stay with us, and also to get pills to cure mum's illness.)

He went on: "Because I was only there for a short time, they couldn't get an exact fix on my location – that's why it's taken them a while to find me. But now they know which reality I'm in. Once they know that, it's only a matter of time before they catch up with me."

"So it was them who set your alarm off back home, then?" I asked.

"Apparently so. How close they were I don't know – the alarm only tells me they're within ten miles or so. They could've DARTed right into the next street, for all I can tell."

"So they can trace us here, too?" asked Jake.

"Sadly, once they're in this reality they can trace us through the DARTs wherever we go," said Sam.

"So why don't we get rid of them?" asked mum. I hadn't thought of that.

Sam sighed again. "If only it were that simple, Heather," he said. "I could throw them in a ditch, yeah, but that would mean we'd never be able to use them again if we needed to escape. And, as I told you before, anyone who's used the DARTs has traces of radiation on them which they can detect, too." He glanced at Jake and I, who had both used the DARTs to travel to another reality. "So it's not just me, but Jake and Ethan who they'll be following."

Jake stared at him. This was the first he'd heard of the radiation thing. "Radiation?" he said in a squeak.

Sam managed a faint smile. "It's OK, it's harmless – just a left-over trace from going through inter-reality space.

"But don't forget these people mean business. They're not coming just to give me a slap on the wrist. The best we can hope for if they catch us is they take me back for trial and leave the boys alone."

"And the worst?" said mum.

Sam looked her in the eye, then shifted his gaze, as if he couldn't bear to say it to her. In a small voice he said: "They decide none of us are worth the effort of taking back home, and they… deal with us all here."

"Deal with us?" I asked.

Sam looked sadly at me. "Well…" he said, then stopped.

I knew what he meant, and it appeared the others did, too. "Deal with" meant kill.

Mum put her head in her hands and Jake and I sat stunned. I remember Sam had said the bosses at I-ART were notorious for shooting first and asking questions later, but I hadn't believed, until now, that they could be so ruthless.

"But Jake and I are no threat to them, are we?" I asked, rather desperately. My voice was a bit higher than normal.

"Neither am I, Ethan," said Sam sadly. "Although I've committed a crime, they could let me live here forever and never hear from me again. But they don't think like that. They want to punish me for doing wrong, and they may want to punish you by association. At the very least they'll want to find out what you know about me – and they'll be quite pleased to recover the DARTs I took. They cost millions to manufacture."

At this point his voice started to break, and he put his hands over his face. Through his fingers, we could just hear him saying: "I'm so, so sorry. I should never have come into your lives."

Mum got up and went over to Sam, putting her arms around him. "Hey, hey," she whispered soothingly, as if to a child. "It's not your fault, come on... we can't give up yet."

Ever since Sam had brought mum the pills that would change her life, curing her of the illness she had suffered since she threw my abusive dad out of the house some years ago, I had seen such a big difference in her.

For the previous four years I had assumed the role of parent in the house – both to little Lizzie and mum herself – cooking, cleaning, shopping; everything, in fact. But since her miraculous cure (doctors in our reality didn't even believe her ME, or chronic fatigue, was real) she had become the mum I remembered from long ago. Strong, capable, fun, loving, confident – all of these and more.

So Sam had not only become my new father figure, but had actually given me my mum back. There was no way I regretted him coming into our lives.

I got up and joined mum in hugging Sam now. “We owe you so much,” I said to him. “It’s not your fault they’re after you. We’ll do all we can to help you stay free.” Mum smiled at me proudly, and Sam grinned through his tears.

“You’re a good boy, Ethan,” he said, not for the first time.

I broke off the hug and sat down again.

“So,” I said. “What’s the plan?”

Lessons

We spent the rest of that day – our last in the barn, though we didn't know it then – trying to figure out a way of getting I-ART to leave us in peace.

We all came up with solutions. Some were unworkable, like Jake's idea about going to the police ("They'll think we're mad," said mum); some were worth considering, like mine about swapping the car for a motorhome and spending the foreseeable future travelling round the country so they couldn't get a fix on us ("Maybe after a few weeks they'll give up!" I said, hopefully); and others were downright daft, like Lizzie's suggestion that we fly to another country to escape them.

As mum pointed out, we didn't exactly have lots of spare money to spend on plane tickets, and they could just as easily follow us to another country if they really wanted to, anyway.

"We have planes in our reality, too, Lizzie,"

smiled Sam.

"And chocolate?" she asked.

"And chocolate. Though it's not as nice as yours."

Lizzie seemed pleased with this, and went back to dressing her teddy in some of her clothes.

By the afternoon we'd come to the conclusion that we would just have to sit it out in the barn – we were safer there than running around the country – but be ready to get in the car and leave as soon as the alarm went off again. Presuming it meant they were within ten miles of us, we would have some time at least to pack up and leave, but we decided to get a lot of stuff ready, just in case. Where we'd go next we had no idea, though Sam reckoned he had a few places in mind.

The idea of running again didn't appeal to any of us, but it was our only option. We couldn't go home yet – by now they'd have traced the DARTs' radiation back to our house – so we'd just have to sit tight until they gave up. Sam believed they'd not have the financial backing to spend months running after us, and would be recalled sooner rather than later.

“Our worth to them is limited,” he explained. “Sure, they want to recover the DARTs, and me, but if it’s going to cost them too much manpower to do it they won't bother.”

I thought at the time this sounded like wishful thinking, but didn’t say anything. After all, we were all hoping we’d be able to go home soon. Jake, in particular, was missing his family and worried they’d tell the authorities if he wasn’t home by the time school started next week. And then we’d have to worry about the police being after us, as well. What a mess this all was!

That afternoon Sam insisted we all find out how to operate the DARTs properly – “just in case,” he said – so he sat us all down and showed us how to programme them.

Sam’s and Duncan’s DARTs were strikingly similar. Though from different realities they were, of course, the same basic technology. Small and pebble-like, the devices fitted easily in the palm of your hand

and felt smooth yet heavy, like lead. They seemed to give off a faint glow, and the surface was a shiny, silvery colour that reflected the colours of the rainbow, like hologramatic wrapping paper.

Although both Jake and I had used the DARTs before, we only knew how to find and press the nearly invisible button which activated them (the first time I'd used it had been by accident). We hadn't needed to programme them, as the DART we used took us to Sam's reality and back automatically – they have a failsafe device, which means you always return home after a trip unless you've programmed it otherwise.

Now, however, Sam wanted to show us how to programme in a specific universe, thereby overriding the 'return' button.

Holding the device in finger and thumb by its more pointed ends, he pressed lightly, as though squeezing a lemon. As soon as he did, the DART seemed to open up like a flower or a cracked egg, top and bottom folding out to reveal the inner workings of the device. Inside was a small numbered dial, like you see on brief-cases or padlocks that need a combination to get into. Each of the 12 numbers, black on a white background, was only a couple of millimetres high.

"This," said Sam, "is where you programme in the reality code you want to go to. All you do is spin the numbers round with your nail, and you can go to any of millions of realities. The important thing, of course, is to know what number your own particular reality is."

Jake and I leant forward to see better. The number showing on the dial was 367,930,509,022. "I want you all to memorise that number," he said.

"You what?" said Jake.

Sam laughed. "It's not that difficult, really," he said. "You memorise numbers that long all the time – mobile phone numbers are about the same length."

"No," said Jake, "I meant why?"

Sam went serious again. "That's my home reality. I need you to remember it – and your own – in case anything happens and we get separated. I also need you to memorise one more – my contact Damien's phone number, so if you ever need to, you can get help from someone who would do anything to save your lives."

Mum went white, and Lizzie declared she could never in a million years learn numbers that long ("That's a million gazillion!" she shouted, incredulous.) But after much repetition, and plenty of hard thinking, by the end of the day we had all memorised Sam's reality, our own (367,930,671,552, in case you're interested) and Damien's phone number, plus the coded message that would bring us his help (Simply: 'Devil's Bridge.' Why, Sam wouldn't tell us: "It'll take too long," he said.)

"You see how your reality code number has the same first six digits as my own," Sam explained that afternoon, as we had been reciting them together.

"Why is that?" asked mum.

"It's because our reality and Sam's reality are quite close together," said Jake.

Sam nodded. I told you Jake was clever. "Yeah,"

he said. "The closer the number, the more similar the realities are to each other. So one with just one number more than yours, say, may only have a few tiny differences. You could live there for years and never find out what that difference is."

"So realities with really different numbers would be totally different, then," said mum.

"Precisely," went on Sam. "Those still with dinosaurs have six noughts at the beginning – they diverged really early on in history."

By this time it was beginning to get dark, and as we had no electric light, only candles and torches, to see by, we decided to try and relax for a while. Mum put the tea on – tinned hotdogs, peas and carrots and baby potatoes – while Sam finished off putting some of our gear into the car, ready in case we had to leave in a hurry. He left us just with a rucksack each, filled with essentials, which he told us to keep packed and near us at all times.

"Keep it ready in case we have to run," he said. "We don't want to have to wait while you look for your toothbrush, Ethan."

"Whaddyoumean?" I mumbled. I was tired, and fed up with this situation, to be honest. Jake laughed. "He never brushes his teeth anyway," he said. I threw a pack of cards at him. It was the only thing to hand.

"Ow," he said, as it hit him on the arm.

"That was an ace," I grinned.

"Oh ha ha ha." Jake rubbed his arm. "That's gonna bruise." "Girl," I went on.

Mum shouted over "Cut it out you two" from her seat by the stove, where Lizzie was helping her stir the pan. "This is almost done."

"Oh good," I said. "What is it today, mother? Foie gras with pickled duck, pea puree and a herb and lavender jus?"

Mum laughed. "Just be grateful you've got food," she said. Boy, those words would come back to haunt me not long afterwards.

Later that evening we were all lying in our sleeping bags, trying to doze off and – apart from Lizzie, who was softly snoring – failing miserably. Me and

Jake had moved some way away from the others, liking to have our own space, while mum, Sam and Lizzie were closer to the door.

After a while we started to talk, as we all agreed we weren't yet tired enough to get to sleep. None of us knew, or cared, what time it was. We kept our voices low, so as not to disturb my sister.

Sam had given Jake one of the DARTs, so he could practise setting the dial, and he was playing with it as we spoke, turning the numbers round with his nail, fascinated at the prospect of being transported into another world again.

"Sam," said Jake after a while, "tell us about the time you met Damien."

Sam hesitated. "I don't think it's a tale I should tell just before we get to sleep," he said. "It might give you nightmares."

"Oh go on," said Jake, but mum interrupted, forever the sensible one: "Not tonight, Jake."

Instead, Sam started to tell us more about a time he'd DARTed into a reality where the dinosaurs had never faced extinction, so humans and most other animals we would recognise had not even evolved.

"Were they like the ones you see in books?" I asked. Like many kids, I had been fascinated by dinosaurs at one stage, and was familiar with the more commonly known ones.

"Not the same," said Sam. "Remember, they'd had millions of years to evolve. They were still dinosaurs as we'd recognise them, though. Their evolutionary path hadn't taken them much farther."

"Were there no animals you recognised then?" This was Jake, still twirling the DART dial. "What about mammals? Didn't they only evolve in our reality because the dinosaurs died off?"

Sam replied: "To be frank, Jake, I wasn't there long enough to do a survey." I laughed. "I took a few readings about atmosphere, water, etc, had a quick scoot around, took some photographs and left. It was too dangerous to stay more than a couple of days."

"But you did see some dinosaurs, right?" Jake wasn't going to let this one go.

Sam pulled his sleeping bag higher up around his neck – it was getting colder – and shuddered. “Oh yes, there were hundreds of them. Everywhere you looked. Small ones, big ones, fat ones, flying ones, narky ones, placid ones, green ones, blue ones, orange ones…”Mum started giggling, and then…

BEEP… BEEP… BEEP… BEEP… BEEP… BEEP… BEEP… BEEP

It was Sam’s alarm. They were coming for us.

Leaving

Immediately we all began to panic. Sam swore loudly, mum leant over to Lizzie and shook her awake, I struggled to get out of my sleeping bag and grab my rucksack full of essentials, and Jake got his feet caught in a blanket and fell off the boxes he'd been lying on. He landed with a thump on the dusty floor.

Sam was trying to get his stuff together while shouting instructions at the rest of us, but no-one was really paying him much attention; we were all too busy trying to get ourselves ready to run – again.

I had managed to put on my shoes – I was already wearing jeans, a t-shirt and a hoodie, as being fully clothed in bed was the norm – when Jake joined me, trainers in his hand.

"Don't forget your rucksack," he said, pointing to the bag near my feet.

"I wasn't going to," I said, irritated and scared. "Put your shoes on, you can't go anywhere without shoes." Jake sat down heavily on what had just been my bed and did as I told him.

I looked over to where mum was trying to wake a sleepy Lizzie. Sam was putting on his coat, and staring around him a bit wildly as if he didn't know quite what to do next. I think, despite all the preparation, this had come a bit suddenly.

"We have to go, now!" he was saying. "They could be just round the corner."

As he spoke, there was a sound over by the doorway. In hindsight, I don't think Sam or mum heard it, and I wish I had warned them. But it wouldn't have been any use, anyway. The agents were already at the door. It would have been pointless for us to try to escape.

Instinctively, I grabbed Jake and pushed him further towards the back of the barn, where there were plenty of boxes and bits of old machinery to hide behind.

"Get down!" I hissed at him, and my friend and I crouched down in the dark.

Peering over the top of an old broken engine, I watched, helpless, as mum, Lizzie and Sam started running for the door – right into the arms of a group of burly men with powerful torches.

There were about six or seven of them, all large, muscular and tall, dressed in black and carrying what looked like handguns.

Jake and I held our breath, barely daring to look, as the agents grabbed my family before they could leave the barn. They were shouting something I didn't quite catch, although I did hear mum yelling "Leave us alone!" Lizzie was crying. It was heartbreaking.

"What do we do?" whispered Jake. He sounded as frightened as I was. I didn't have an answer.

I watched as two of the agents came towards us, searching around them in the dark, their powerful torches sweeping over the boxes, abandoned sleeping bags and dirty dinner dishes left over from that evening's last meal.

As they got nearer, Jake's hand gripped my arm

tighter and tighter, leaving what would later be a rather impressive series of finger-shaped bruises, and his breathing got louder and louder. I swear I could hear my heartbeat pounding in my chest.

One of the agents was getting closer to our hiding place, and I knew it wouldn't be very long before we were found. What would happen to us then?

I didn't have to worry about that, however.

As the agent came nearer, and his torchlight picked out the forms of two scared boys hiding in the dark, Jake took a decision he was later to regret.

Panicked, he pressed the button on the DART he had been holding, sending us both into darkness.

....

When we opened our eyes we were crouching on a mossy hill.

It was just after sunrise, so the light was thin and feeble, but we could still see we were in a totally alien world to the one we had 'just' left.

The sky was a mixture of orange, yellow and bright green, the vegetation was immensely thick, tall trees and ferns stabbing the sky, like a rainforest, and the very air seemed different – fresh, icy; like the air you get at the top of a mountain or by the seaside on a cold winter's day.

"Where… where are we?" My voice was barely a whisper. My throat was dry and sore.

Jake looked down at the DART he was clutching tightly in his fist, and out of the corner of my eye I saw his mouth open and shut like a goldfish, several times. Even in the middle of my terror, I had found it funny.

He shook his head, as if to clear his thoughts, and muttered something I didn't catch as he stood up, wincing in pain.

I turned away with difficulty from the strange sight before me – the dripping trees, ferns, orange-red sky, where odd birds were wheeling around like vultures – and stood up too, groaning at the aches in my legs. Jake was standing right next to me, one hand clutching the DART. A rucksack was on his shoulder, but was beginning to slide off. His mouth was still open. “What?” I said then. Again, I only whispered.

Jake looked me in the eye, his own eyes scared. “I… I just pressed the DART… to get away…” he faltered.

“Yes,” I said, “but where are we?” I had recovered a little, and a thought occurred to me. “You sent us to another reality – but which one?”

Jake looked stupidly at the DART in his hand, then put it in his hoodie pocket.

Slowly, he said: “I had been putting in reality numbers with six zeroes at the front – remember Sam told us those were the ones where dinosaurs had never been made extinct, as they diverged from our own universe so very long ago?” I nodded, amazed. “And I didn’t have time to change it – I couldn’t have seen anyway, not in the dark, the numbers are so small… so I just pressed the button…”

“And now we’re in the land of the dinosaurs,” I said, in wonder, looking around us again.

"Yup," said Jake, putting his rucksack down and rubbing his arms, "I reckon it took us a long time to get here, by the feel of things."

I realised my arms, legs and back were all aching, the way they do when you've been standing or sitting a long time, and remembered that although DARTing from one reality to another felt like it only took a moment, it really took a varied amount of time. The longer away you were from your own world, the longer it took.

When we had fled from the agents back in the barn it had been nearly dark, say just after six in the evening – here it looked like dawn.

"I reckon we've been DARTing for around 12 hours or so," said Jake, confirming my thoughts. "So back home…" he stopped, and looked at me, worry on his face.

"Back home, the agents have taken mum, Lizzie and Sam to… well, we don't know where, do we? They could be back in Sam's reality. They could still be in ours, waiting for us to return. Or they could…"

It was my turn to stop, and tears came to my eyes. I blinked them back in.

I didn't want to finish that sentence. Sam had hinted that the agents may just want to kill us, but I didn't want to think about that.

"Anyway," Jake said, "we should really DART back straight away. If we do that we'll have been gone a whole day. If we don't move we'll end up back in the barn, and we can see if there's any clues as to what's happened to the others."

It wasn't much of a plan, but it was the best we had. We'd have to go back at some point, and the longer we left it the less likely we were to find out where the others had been taken.

"OK," I said, picking my rucksack up again, "but first let me take a few photos of this place – it's awe-some." And I dug out my phone from my rucksack front pocket, turned it on (back in the barn we had kept them turned off to preserve the batteries) and started to snap the scenery. Although mobiles did not usually work as phones in different realities, it seemed the cameras still did.

Jake had been doing the same, and was mid-selfie when I heard a low growl behind me. Turning around, I saw the most amazing yet terrifying sight I had ever seen.

Emerging out of a patch of ferns was a large, lizard-like animal. About the size of a cow, it looked a little like a Komodo dragon, with scaly grey skin and a forked tongue flicking out of its mouth, but there the similarity ended; it had six legs, not four, each one ending in a mass of long, curved claws, and its tail was curled over its back, like a scorpion's, with a massive sting on the end, too. A hissing, growling noise was coming from its mouth, and its small eyes were dead, black and stupid.

Needless to say, we ran like the wind. I think I may have been screaming, for good measure.

And I'm pretty sure that's when the DART fell out of Jake's pocket.

Lost

We ran for a long time. I can't tell you exactly how long, because really we've been running ever since, but I remember my rucksack banging against my back, the tins of food in there hurting with every jolt.

I remember leaping over streams of water, pushing through rows of ferns and being smacked in the face by numerous overhanging branches.

I remember Jake being up ahead, his little, jeans-clad legs going faster than I'd seen them ever before, and then, panting, trying to shout at him to stop – stop, because we didn't know where we were going.

Finally I came to a halt, leant against a mossy green tree trunk and put my rucksack on the ground. It would take a while before I got my breath back.

Jake was a little way ahead. I saw him also put his rucksack on the floor and then fall to his knees.

"Jee-sus," he was saying through his panting. "What in the name of Justin Bieber *was* that thing?"

I shook my head. "A dinosaur?" I offered. My sides were hurting with the effort of running. I had never been a runner; my 100m at school took about three times as long as everyone else's. Jake was the same.

"That was no dinosaur," said my friend, lying down and putting his hand on his chest as if to check his heartbeat. We were in a small clearing, and the ground was covered in soft, yellowy-green plants. It wasn't grass, exactly, but not far off.

"Well," I said, my breath beginning to return, "you're forgetting we haven't gone back in time, so the dinosaurs here are unlikely to look anything like what we think of as dinosaurs."

"Of course," said Jake, and he sat up. As I said, he's the clever one – it's just sometimes he forgets this. "Of course," he repeated, as if he'd had a brain-wave. "Our dinosaurs, back in our reality, died out around 65 million years ago. Here, they didn't. Hell, that's a lo-o-ong time to be evolving."

I was impressed by his knowledge, but didn't tell

him. “So,” I said, wanting to show I was intelligent too, “they’ve evolved into completely different species, and…”

“And we’re unlikely to come across a Tyrannosaurus Rex,” finished Jake.

“That’s just as well,” I commented, picking up my rucksack again. There was sweat dripping down my back. “Anyway, I think we’d better DART back home now. We’ve run quite a long way, which means we won’t be very close to the barn anymore, and we don’t want to get any farther, or we’ll get lost.”

Jake was getting up too, looking around nervously for any more creatures. His hand was in his pocket. “Yeah,” he said. “The sooner we DART home the sooner we can find out what happened to the others.”

I went and stood next to him, waiting. In order to DART from universe to universe you had to press the DART button, and whatever and whoever you were in contact with at the time would transport with you.

Jake had started to look worried, and I noticed he was searching more and more frantically in his hoodie pockets. There were only two of them, and he appeared to have looked in them several times each.

"Don't tell me," I said, realising what he was doing and beginning to panic. "Please, just don't tell me…" Jake stopped searching his pockets and started scanning the ground instead. He dropped to his knees again and felt around with both hands, like you would if you lost a contact lens on the carpet.

"It was in my pocket, Ethan; it was in my pocket." His voice had started to rise.

"OK," I said, "let's not panic just yet. Let me help you look."

So we looked. We took Jake's hoodie off and searched all his clothes, inside and out. We looked on the ground all around, but of course the plants were really thick, anyway, and it was like looking for a dropped pin on an overgrown lawn.

After an hour of looking, we panicked.

……………………………………………

We spent a lot of time searching for the DART, trying to trace our (running) steps back to where we first appeared, hoping at any minute we'd see its shiny, round surface glinting up at us from the ground.

We both knew it was pretty useless to keep looking – the DART could have fallen out anywhere during that first sprint from the monster, and we didn't know exactly which route we'd taken, anyway. We thought we'd found the original spot once, but weren't so sure – everywhere looked the same.

Have you ever been lost in a forest? It's a complete nightmare, I can tell you. Every tree looks the same, you can't tell which way is which and you get disorientated really quickly. It's very easy to be going round in circles and not realise it.

That first day was really hard. We spent hours looking at the ground, stopping only when we were exhausted, to eat and drink a little – thankfully we did have a little food in our rucksacks – before going on again. Jake kept crying, and I pretended not to notice.

I knew he blamed himself, but I didn't. It was an accident.

At least we managed to find water – there was plenty of *that* around, in streams, ponds, puddles and lakes; we had water bottles in our rucksacks, so could fill them up when needed. We found the water – well, the running water, at any rate – amazingly clear and sharp. Jake at first cautioned it may be poisonous to us somehow, but once the water we'd brought with us ran out (which was pretty quick, because it was so hot, and we were drinking a lot) we decided we'd have to risk it. It appeared to be fine – anyway, it was either drink it or die.

Thankfully, apart from insects (which I tried not to look at too closely) and bird-like creatures high up in the sky, we didn't come across any other animals that day. But when it began to get dark we knew we had to find somewhere safe to rest, so we were happy to find a tree we could climb. Its branches were regular, the lowest ones just off the ground, and we hauled ourselves up about ten feet or so until we felt a bit safer.

"Of course, there's bound to be creatures that can climb, or that live in the trees," said Jake. His voice was small, and I didn't want to upset him more, or I would have punched him for pointing this out. I don't think either of us slept at all that night.

On the second day we resumed our search, trying hard to remember which way we had run through the jungle.

"I think I remember jumping over that stream," I said at one point, "there, where that muddy patch is on the other side. I slipped in it a bit." But when we looked there was no skid mark, no footprint, so we had to conclude it was the wrong stream.

"I remember that funny-looking bush," said Jake at another clearing, pointing at a decidedly odd, red-leaved, low shrub which had spiky orange flowers sticking up at all angles. It appeared to be covered with buzzing, black insects, much bigger than any flies I had ever seen. We didn't get any closer.

"OK, so which way then?" I sighed, my eyes, as

ever, searching all around just in case the DART was there.

"I... that way," said my friend, heading off between two thin trees with black bark. I wasn't so sure, but followed him anyway. We pushed through some thick vegetation and found ourselves next to a large pond. It was oval, with purple plants floating on its surface and a grey slime around its edges.

We hadn't come across a pond before, so we knew we had been heading the wrong way. Jake stopped, turned around rather wildly and suddenly burst into tears. "We'll never get back," he wailed. "It's all my fault. If only I'd kept hold of the DART and not put it in my pocket. It's useless. We're stuck here, and we're going to die... I WANT MY MUM!"

Crying myself by this point, I grabbed Jake and, although I'd never hugged him before, despite him being my best friend, hugged him until he stopped wailing.

We both sat on the ground, by the edge of the pond, and cried silently for a while. Hey, don't laugh

– I bet you would have done the same, and don't forget we were only 11.

We didn't cry for long, however, as after about five minutes we heard a splashing noise coming from the pond. Looking back, we saw a huge creature resembling a crocodile pulling itself out of the water, grey slime clinging to its thick, scaly legs.

"Jeez, Louise," Jake sighed, as we quickly got to our feet and ran back the way we had come. By the time we were far enough away to stop we were laughing. I think it may have been hysteria, but I wasn't complaining – it was better than crying, any day.

After that we made sure we were armed. We each found a dead branch, big enough to hurt something but small and light enough to carry. And we got ourselves a bit more organised, checking what we had in our packs and sharing them out into rations for each small meal.

"Why the hell did Sam pack tins of food but no tin opener?" asked Jake, throwing a useless tin of beans to the floor in annoyance.

"I don't expect he reckoned on us being stranded in a tin opener-less world," I said, repacking the few spare clothes I'd taken out. "I've got a first aid kit," I said brightly, holding up a small pouch which contained antiseptic, a bandage and the usual odds and ends.

"Oh great; next time a crocodile comes at us you can put a plaster on his jaws; that'll stop him taking your arm off."

I laughed a little at that, but it wasn't funny really.

That afternoon we encountered a pack of creatures for the first time. We were walking along a natural pathway between trees, looking on the ground for the DART even though we were pretty sure we hadn't come this way before, when I heard a noise behind us.

I stopped. "Jake," I hissed. He stopped too, a little way in front. "What?" he asked.

Before I could say anything there was a deep growling from the side, and a creature leapt out of a patch of leaves.

It was about as big as a large dog, sort of furry and

with four legs, but more rounded than any dog I'd ever seen, with a huge belly, a large head and a big, gaping mouth like a fish. I didn't have much time to examine what it looked like, to be honest, before it was followed by another, and another. They were obviously a little unsure of us – they'd never seen a human before, presumably – so didn't attack at first, but we didn't wait for them to decide to act.

"Run!" Jake and I both shouted simultaneously. Well, no-one needed to tell me twice. I was getting kind of good at running. Leaping over a log, I looked behind, and saw at least three or four of the creatures coming after us. They were sort of lolloping along, rather than running. I'd seen nature documentaries; I knew what normally happened in situations like this. And I wasn't very keen on becoming a square meal.

Jake was a little way ahead, pushing his way through thick undergrowth, and I was in danger of losing him. My breath was beginning to sound laboured, and I had a stitch already. I could hear the animals behind us, but thankfully they appeared to be getting further away.

We ran on for around ten minutes, which was longer than I think I've ever run in my life, before Jake suddenly veered to the left and started climbing a tree. "Up here!" he panted, and I followed, hauling myself up onto a branch next to my friend.

We sat there, out of breath, and waited for the creatures to appear. My rucksack had been dangling below the branch, and after a minute I pulled it up.

"How do you know they can't climb trees?" I asked, when my breath had returned.

"I don't," said Jake, still panting. "Just an educated guess."

Twenty minutes later we felt it was probably safe to get down. The creatures had obviously given up the chase some time ago – there'd been no sound nor sight of them.

I turned onto my knees in order to lower myself to the ground, when I saw it, behind us.

"Jake!" I shouted, excited, "look at that!"

My friend turned his head, as I pointed behind our

tree towards a clearing some 50 feet away. There, standing looking placidly in our direction, a purple plant sticking out of its mouth, was a long-necked dinosaur.

A real-life, recognisable, absolutely-bloody-huge, brontosaurus-like dinosaur.

That '*true*' dinosaur – the first one we could recognise as being such – was the first of many. On the third day of our adventure in what we began to call Dinoworld (Jake's idea – I completely disown it), we saw dozens.

Climbing a rough hill of rocks at one point, in order to try and get our bearings, we stared down past the jungle onto a broad, flat area with less ferns and trees and more grassy plants. It was like looking at one of the illustrations in a book I had as a little kid. There were about ten of the brontosaurus-like creatures we'd seen the day before, munching away on the plants, their long necks swaying from side to side like a dance.

Some of them were huge, much bigger than any animal I'd ever seen before, while others, presumably the babies, were about as big as a cow. They were a bright green colour, with greyish streaks along their backs.

Behind these there was a herd of other, smaller, dark brown dinosaurs, maybe a dozen of them, with six short legs, curly horns on their heads and long tails which touched the ground. Above them, in the clear, china blue sky, wheeled huge bird-like animals which we only ever saw in silhouette. To be honest, I didn't want to see them up close.

We had two near misses that day, as we wandered aimlessly around, now not having the slightest hope of finding the DART but looking all the same.

The first time we surprised a lizard-like animal as we walked through a thick clump of trees. About the size of a lion, it had six legs, like the first one we'd seen, but was obviously a different species, with a head like a rhinoceros, all scales and armour plating. It turned on us as we stopped, unsure what to do, and came at us at surprising speed, mouth open to reveal several rows of teeth, like a shark.

Instead of running this time we stood our ground, yelled and swung at it with our branch-club weapons.

I'm pretty sure neither of us actually hit it, but thankfully it retreated.

The second time was more serious. We were sitting on the ground, packing away after a small meal of biscuits and the last of the raisins, when there was a rustling noise behind Jake. I was facing him, and saw a creature leap over a low-lying, spikey-leaved bush about six feet away.

This one looked like a cross between an ostrich and one of those small but terrifying predator dinosaurs they have in all the movies – Jake later told me it was a lot like a velociraptor, one of the most vicious creatures imaginable.

It had two long legs with five-toed feet ending in long, sharp claws, startlingly green feathers on its back and belly and short arms, again ending in long claws. A long neck ended in a bird-like head with a yellow crest on the back and a beak-like mouth, which was opened in a screeching scream. The monster was about as tall as me, and looked even hungrier.

"Jake!" I squeaked, but he had already spotted my

horrified expression and knew something nasty had appeared. We quickly got up, grabbed our bags and shouldered them, so we could handle our weapons more easily.

"Stand by me," I panted, and Jake came to my side. We stood, unsure what to do next, our clubs in our hands, ready.

The creature looked at us stupidly, moving its head from side to side as if to see us better. It had small, black eyes with very little intelligence behind them. Sam was right, I thought, these dinosaurs had evolved very little over millions of years.

Just as I was beginning to think it would leave us alone it screeched again, and all of a sudden another three appeared, landing in the small clearing next to their brother.

I was already hot – our hoodies were tied round our waists, as there was no room in our rucksacks, and we had been baking in the heat – but now I felt sweat run down my forehead and past my eyebrows. I shook it away without taking my eyes off the quartet of dinosaurs before us.

"What do we do now?" I asked quietly. There seemed little point running, as they had longer legs than we did and would surely be on us as soon as we turned away from them.

"Well," said Jake, and I could hear the fear in his voice, "I think we might have to stand and fight this one out, Ethan old chap." Jake always sounded flippant when he was scared. He did the same once when we had to fight the bullies in primary school.

But these were no bullies; these were creatures from another world: hungry, vicious creatures at that. And anyway, we'd lost to the bullies, going home with bruises our mothers would cry over.

I was loath to fight – I'd never been any good at it. But the decision was taken out of my hands, when one of the monsters leapt at Jake, its thin, scaly legs in front of it as if in a karate kick. Without thinking I swung at it with my club, hitting it by chance rather than design, and knocked it to the floor two feet away, dazed.

Suddenly all was madness. The three other animals leapt at us, and our whole world became a pecking, clawing, hitting and biting frenzy.

I was lashing out blindly with my club, and Jake was doing the same. I think I hit one in the face, but I can't be sure. Jake definitely got one square in the body, and it went screeching away into the undergrowth, while another pecked my arm and drew blood. I was grunting and yelling, while Jake was calm, lashing out as one of the creatures came too close.

They weren't easily put off, however, and it took us until we were close to exhaustion before they all decided we weren't worth the effort and left us alone. As the last one leapt away, blood dripping from a wound on its belly, Jake and I dropped to the floor, chests heaving, t-shirts soaked with sweat and cuts bleeding. I wiped an arm across my forehead. It came away with blood smeared across it.

"We've got to get out of this place," I said,

bleakly.

Jake nodded, too tired to speak.

A couple of minutes went by, both of us lost in our own thoughts, then I struggled to my feet, sighed, and picked up my rucksack, which had been flung to the ground during the fight. It was still heavy with the useless tins. "Hey, this would make a pretty good weapon as well," I said, lugging it onto my shoulder. "Come on, I need a wash. Let's go back to that stream we saw back there."

The next second I was pushed to the ground by something heavy. My bag went flying, my left arm got bent underneath me and I fell heavily onto my side, face planted into the ground. The earth smelled like flowerpots.

I heard Jake shouting and tried to get up, but there was something sitting on my left hip. It was digging into my side. I managed to turn my head and saw one of the creatures had returned. Obviously it was hungry enough to have a second go at making me dinner.

Petrified and unable to move, I saw its grey-yellow

beak, about a foot away from my face, open into a screech before it pulled back its head as if to strike. I could see its pink tongue. I shut my eyes and waited for the pain.

There was a 'thwack,' and I heard Jake swear as he smashed the club into the creature's neck and it screeched once more before falling off my side and into the dirt.

I scrambled away, still unable to find my feet, and kicked out at it as it lay on the ground.

"Jee-sus!" I panted, rubbing my arm, my side and leg in turn. They all hurt. I looked at the monster, lying on the ground. There was blood coming out of its mouth. It was not moving.

"Jee-sus!" I said again. I was unable to say anything more eloquent.

Jake was crouched on his heels, the home-made weapon still in both hands. There was blood on it, too. Suddenly he leapt to his feet, went over to the creature and began hitting it with the club. Feathers flew up.

After four or five strikes I got up, went over to him

and grabbed him from behind. He stopped immediately, dropping his weapon.

"It's OK, Jake," I said, slowly. "I think it's dead."

Dozing

Jake was asleep. His curly blond hair was over his eyes, so I couldn't see if they were closed, but I could hear the slow, heavy breathing of someone who was deeply entrenched in dreamland. Lucky swine. He was beginning to snore a little, too.

Despite the jealousy, I was glad. We'd barely slept these last three days, what with all the worry, the hunger… and the running, of course.

I looked for a moment at his hair, and sighed quietly. It was beginning to look dirty and a bit matted (we didn't have a brush between us; one thing we didn't think we'd miss, but… you never realise what you'll need until you haven't got it). Jake was always so meticulous about his hair.

I used to laugh at him, making fun of how he washed it every day, curled his fingers through it when he was anxious, and wouldn't let anyone cut it too short. Well now it was having a chance to grow, I thought. If his mum could see him now, she'd go spare…

I shifted my weight. The ferns, put there to try and make our perch a bit comfier, were beginning to dig into my backside, which had never been particularly meaty but was now thinner than ever. I didn't think I'd ever get used to sleeping up a tree. Hell, I hoped I wouldn't have to do it much longer. Maybe tomorrow we'd find the DART and be able to get back home.

Home. Thinking about it made me cry, but that was OK – Jake was asleep, he couldn't see me. I wiped my eyes with my sleeve. My hoodie was decidedly dirty, too – it was smeared with mud, from where we'd slipped into an insect-filled hole while running away from the beasts. Jake's had blood on it, too, I noticed. I don't know whose blood it was. His or… the monster's.

We still hadn't come up with any names for them, the creatures that filled this alien land – I refused to call most of them dinosaurs; it was just too weird. There were too many of them to think up names – all we'd done so far was decide that there were two types: harmless ones, and those that wanted to eat us.

Thankfully, there appeared to be considerably more harmless, vegetarian creatures than ravenous, man-eating ones. I suppose that mirrored our own world, really – after all, grass-eating herbivores far outnumber the carnivores, don't they?

Like cows or deer in our world, here the herbivores walked around in herds, munching away placidly on plants, while the carnivores hunted either singly or in packs, like tigers or wolves.

I shuddered. The packs were the worst. A lone creature could be fought off pretty easily, with a bit of courage and a big stick (I subconsciously checked on my chosen weapon, stuck into a crevice between two branches, close enough to grab if needed. I'd chosen it well – it was thick and not too long, so was easy to hit with). After all, these creatures had never seen human beings before, so weren't even sure if we were edible. Single ones seemed to be more afraid of us… unless they were especially hungry, I supposed.

The packs, though, were another matter. They had no fear, and were very good at creeping up on you when your back was turned. We'd barely survived that day's encounter. If it wasn't for Jake I'd not be sat there now, listening to him snore.

Poor Jake. He'd only come to our house for a sleepover, for a couple of days of playing computer games and eating crisps and pizza, and he'd ended up first running away from we didn't know what, to living in a bare barn for five days and now…

Now we were stuck in an alien land, with no hope of going home.

I drifted off to sleep, and had a dream in which Sam, all scruffy as usual in worn jeans and an old rock t-shirt (The Foo Fighters, I saw dimly), his longish, greying dark hair tumbling into his eyes, was talking to me.

"You're stuffed now, Ethan," Sam said. "The dinosaurs haven't even discovered fire yet. They're really thick. You're not going to get a cup of tea here." He was smiling.

Sam went on: "Did I ever tell you about the world I visited where the Nazis won the Second World War? Man it was awful. You couldn't watch Sesame Street without them throwing propaganda at you. Imagine Big Bird as a Nazi. Incredible. And the currency was covered in pictures of dogs." Then he lifted his arms up to the sky, and a huge, reptile-like bird with fangs dripping blood emerged from his back, where I saw it had been hiding all along…

I woke with a start, as you often do when something disturbing happens in a dream. Shifting my weight, I found my backside had gone numb and something was digging into my left leg. It was still pitch black, so I couldn't even see my hand in front of my face, but I knew what it was – my rucksack, full of tins of food. If only we had thought to pack a tin-opener, I thought for the hundredth time.

My stomach growled. It was nearly empty. We'd barely eaten since we got here – there was a limited amount of food in our two emergency rucksacks, and most of it was in tins, so was useless to us until we found a way to get into them.

Despite rationing quite carefully, we had nearly eaten all the raisins, biscuits, cereal bars and chocolate we had with us. I reckoned we had about another two days' worth left, if we ate like sparrows.

In the three days we'd been in this land of dinosaurs, we hadn't found a single thing we recognised to be edible – not a berry, mushroom, grain of cereal, fruit or vegetable. There seemed to be nothing but thick-trunked trees with massive broad leaves, huge ferns which dripped water constantly, moss and lichens and weird, oddly-shaped and coloured flowers which smelled like rotten meat. It was like being in the middle of a jungle.

And as for the animals… well, they were mostly the stuff of nightmares.

I pulled the rucksack a bit further under my back, so it didn't slip off during the night, and closed my eyes again. For a second the image of Sam releasing the reptile returned, then, thankfully, I slept.

I was awoken by Jake's voice, calling softly from

his own uncomfortable perch. It was a big tree we were on, and we'd positioned ourselves in a large fork which created an almost level platform. It was big enough for the both of us, as well as our meagre possessions.

I opened my eyes and saw it was light. Well, we'd made it through another night at least.

"Ethan," Jake was saying again. He sounded tired.

"Yeah, yeah, I'm awake." I looked at him, his hair messy and his clothes bloody, and suddenly he seemed a lot younger than his 11 years, like a little boy lost. I supposed I did, too.

"Is it time for breakfast already?" I asked. "As long as you're cooking, I'll have bacon, eggs, mushrooms, sausages, fried bread – oh god yes, fried bread – and…"

"Stop it," said Jake, and he sounded like he was going to cry. I shut up. I knew it wasn't funny.

"OK, Jakey boy, what's the plan for today then?" I asked instead. Jake was the clever one, he always had a plan, and I tended to do what he suggested. Usually it was the right thing to do.

Jake opened his rucksack and took out his water bottle, drank from it, shook it to see how much was inside then began rummaging inside his bag again. "Well," he said, "the first thing to do is to have a little to eat, then find some water and fill our bottles."

"Eminently sensible," I said. I'd learnt that phrase from Jake himself, last summer, and enjoyed using it often.

"Elementary, my dear Jones," he replied. I'm not sure that worked, but never mind.

"And then?" I added, as I found my own bottle and took a sip. It was icy cold, although the air was warming up and it looked like it would yet again be a hot and humid day. The insects, some as big as my hand and as weird as a dream, were already buzzing around us.

"And then we continue our quest for the missing DART." He grinned, but there was very little humour in it. His teeth were dirty, too, I noticed. Toothbrushes were another thing we didn't have. We'd forgotten to pack them after all, despite Sam's nagging.

"Exactly how much food do we have left?" I asked, wearily.

Jake climbed down from the tree, stretched, then sat on the ground, emptying out his rucksack. I slowly joined him, and soon the contents of mine were also strewn across the floor.

I had six tins of various food, mostly beans, hot dogs and ham, a first aid kit which was already half empty, a large box of matches and a small packet of dried apricots, which was unopened.

"Erm… if you mean how much food do we have that we can actually eat," he said, piling his tins up to one side – hot dogs and beans featured heavily here, too… oh, and I noticed a tin of tomato soup – "then not a lot."

I rubbed my forehead. I had a headache.

"*Exactly*," I said again.

"OK," said Jake. "A packet of dried apricots, four dry and rather crumby crackers, three squares of melted chocolate, one packet of noodles (curry flavour, no less), and a single Oreo."

"We have nothing to cook the noodles in, Jake, so they don't count," I said.

He picked the packet up from the floor and examined it. "I don't suppose they can be eaten raw, can they?" he asked. I pulled a face. "I don't think so."

"Oh. Well in that case it's a cracker each for breakfast," and he handed me a single square cracker. I nibbled at it. It was dry and stale.

"Good?" he asked, as if he was a chef and I was tasting his latest creation. I looked at him, dirty and dishevelled as he was, his hoodie sprayed with blood and a cut above his eye. I smiled between the crumbs. "It's fabulous," I lied.

"Do you want to start on the apricots?" he asked. I shook my head. Neither of us could stand them, though in a couple of days we reckoned we'd be ravenous enough to eat even those. We were saving them until we were desperate.

Once we'd finished breakfast – well, it didn't take

long – we repacked the rest of our belongings into our bags, filled our water bottles from a nearby stream and headed off into the jungle. We had nothing else to do.

Little did we know that day would be one of the most wondrous and unbelievable of our days in this strange land.

For that was the day we found a friend.

And thought we'd discovered an enemy.

A new friend

As we wandered – by now we were just wandering, with no real aim – we talked about our adventures last summer, when Sam had first come into our lives and our world had literally changed.

Jake was laughing about how we'd stolen Sam's DART when Sam was drunk at mum's birthday party, when he suddenly stopped and shushed me.

I stopped too. "What?" I asked, listening.

Jake was glancing about him, but there was nothing to see except thick vegetation all around us. "I thought I heard someone following us," he whispered.

I peered through the thick trees back the way we had just come. "I can't hear anything," I whispered back. As was always the case in this alien land, there was nothing to be heard except the gentle wind, the loud buzz of insects in the air, the odd trickle of water and occasional screech of some nameless creature killing another nameless creature.

Jake shrugged. "Probably nothing," he said, and we walked on.

Later that day, hot and exhausted with hunger, feeling faint, we found a cool spot near a small waterfall and decided to rest. The air was humid and we'd drunk all of our water already, so we needed to fill up our bottles again.

"We may as well eat lunch here," said Jake, finding a rock to sit on. It was covered in blueish lichen.

"Is it lunchtime already?" I asked, screwing the lid on my water bottle and putting my rucksack down on the ground.

Jake laughed thinly. "I reckon so," he said, "though my watch has stopped working, so I've no idea what time it is."

"Well, my stomach says it's half past one," I said, sitting on the ground and opening my bag. "Time to eat the last of the chocolate, I believe."

Jake went quiet as I fished the three squares of chocolate out of the side pocket of my bag, unwrapped them and looked longingly at their melty brownness. I realised I was salivating as I broke off a piece and handed it to my friend.

He took it, sighed, and started slowly nibbling at it. I did the same with my piece, although it quickly melted all over my finger and thumb and I had to lick it off. There was now one piece left.

I looked up, and saw Jake was staring at it as if in a trance. He loved chocolate – whenever we went anywhere back home he'd always have a bar with him. And this was the last piece we had – the last piece we'd ever have, we thought at the time.

I held it out to him. "Here," I said, "you have it." He hesitated, though I knew he wanted it. "Your need is greater than mine," I added. He smiled, took it and slowly ate it.

"That was the best piece of chocolate I've *ever* had," he said, sadly, as he licked every last bit off his fingers and from around his mouth.

Two minutes later, as we sipped our water, Jake suddenly took one of the tins out of his bag and threw it to the ground. "I'm so hungry," he wailed. "Can't we find a way to get these things open? Surely it's not impossible?"

I sighed. "I suppose we could try hitting them against the rocks again," I said. "Maybe we could put a hole in them."

Jake and I both chose a tin – him hotdogs, me a tin of ham – and started throwing them against the rocks. His was dented almost straight away, its label slipping off, but mine was obviously made of stronger stuff and had barely a scratch by the time we gave up, frustrated and tired.

"What we need is a sharp edge," sighed Jake, as he threw his tin to the ground again.

"Yeah, well, I haven't seen one yet," I said, sitting down on the ground once more, sweat pouring down my back. "All the rocks are round and slippy."

"Well we need to look harder," said my friend, "or else we're going to starve. If only…" But I never got to hear the rest of the sentence, as Jake suddenly leapt to his feet and pointed behind me. "Look out!" he yelled.

I turned around, scared, only to come face-to-face with two beady black eyes, staring at me from behind a broad-leaved plant. I leapt to my feet, looked wildly around for my branch/weapon, couldn't see it anywhere, and backed away from the creature. It hadn't moved, but was still staring at me.

"What is it?" I asked, walking backwards to where Jake stood. He'd found his club, and was holding it in both hands.

"I don't know," said Jake quietly, "but I'm not going to wait around to see if it wants to eat me. Let's pack up and go. I'll keep watching it."

As I gathered our stuff together – I found my club over by the waterfall, where I'd carelessly dropped it earlier – Jake stood watching the creature, which by now had climbed out of the plant and was standing in the clearing, staring at us.

When I'd nearly packed everything I came to stand by Jake again. The creature was worryingly similar to the velociraptor-like dinosaurs we'd had the fight with the day before, although it was a lot smaller

– about the size of a cat – and had red feathers, not green ones. Its long legs ended in chicken-like feet with long claws, and it had small front legs which waved nervously in the air, as if it was knitting an invisible jumper. A long scaly neck ended in a small head with a pointy red beak, and it seemed to have small folded wings on its back.

As we watched, unsure what to do next, it trotted forwards to where Jake's battered but unbroken tin of hotdogs lay. It kicked the tin with its clawed toes, making it roll across the ground towards the waterfall.

"I think it's hungry," whispered Jake.

"Well, if it can get into that it's welcome to it," I said, picking up the tin I'd been trying to open minutes before. "Come on, let's go."

But Jake was rooted to the spot. "Hang on," he said, amazed, "I think it's got a plan."

Not understanding what he meant, I turned to watch the dinosaur, and was astonished to see it had grabbed the tin in both feet, claws digging into the ground, and was now stabbing at its dented side with its sharp beak.

“No way,” I said, as on the second try its beak pierced the tin and brine dripped out onto its toes.

“Way,” Jake breathed, as the dinosaur dropped the tin, lent forwards and used its front claws to prise open the hole until it was big enough to spill the contents onto the ground. It started to gobble up the hot dogs, tilting its head back as each one slid down its throat.

When it had eaten all eight it shook its head, looked at us and squawked like a parrot. Jake and I laughed. “I think we’ve found our tin opener,” said my friend, and he took the tin of ham from my hand and threw it to the ground in front of the creature. “See if you can open that one, too,” he said.

Our new friend quickly obliged, first grabbing the tin in its feet then piercing it with its beak, but this time, before it could open the tin with its claws, Jake boldly shooed it away, grabbed the tin and prised the contents out with his fingers.

“Here,” he said, passing me a chunk of ham. I ate

it quickly, as Jake stuffed a large piece into his mouth, licking his fingers for the jelly. “Oh my god that’s good,” he murmured, as he pulled more out of the ragged hole in the tin’s side.

“I think you’d better give our friend some,” I said, as I took another piece from him. The dinosaur was waiting patiently, just like a dog begging for food, its head moving from side to side as it eyed Jake’s meaty hands. Jake threw it a piece, which it caught in its beak and swallowed whole.

Soon the tin was empty. My stomach actually felt full for the first time since we had got to this strange land, and Jake was moaning in delight as he licked the last of the jelly from his fingers.

“Thanks, friend,” he said to the creature, which, satisfied with its meal as well, I supposed, had settled down close to us on the ground, its long legs folded underneath it like a chicken. It flapped its little wings happily.

When we moved on, a few minutes later, the dinosaur followed us. That was fine – we didn’t want to lose our tin-opener.

"I expect it sees us as a source of easy food," said Jake, as we pushed through some dense undergrowth and it flapped its way past us. "Which is great – as long as we keep feeding it, it will open our tins for us."

I was happier than I'd been for days, and put to the back of my mind the fact we only had a limited number of tins of food with us. They'd only last a week, at most. After that… well, after that we'd starve, probably. But that was in the future.

Now… well, now…

"What the?" Jake had stopped ahead of me, and was pointing at something on the ground. For a moment I thought he'd found the DART, and my heart soared with excitement, but when I caught up with him I saw just what he was pointing at.

On a patch of muddy ground in front of him, next to a large bright yellow flower, was a footprint. The unmistakeable outline of a large boot, complete with criss-cross pattern on the sole. And it was much bigger than my size 6 or Jake's tiny size 4.

It was a man's footprint.

Night visitors

The footprint unnerved us, of course. We spent ages looking in the area for others, but found none, not even our own.

It was unsettling to think we were being watched, or followed, by another human being in this land in which we thought we were alone.

And it was even more worrying as we didn't have a clue who it might be.

"Maybe it's someone come to rescue us," I said, as we rested for a while on a fallen tree. Our new-found dinosaur friend, who we had decided to call Tin-o, short for Tin Opener, came and sat by us.

"Like who?" asked Jake. "The agents wouldn't care if we're lost in another universe – surely they'd be glad we're out of the way."

A cheering thought occurred to me. "It could be Sam!" I nearly shouted, but Jake looked unconvinced. "I don't think Sam's feet are that big," he said, "and anyway, wouldn't he have been shouting our names if he was here looking for us?

"Surely we'd have heard him?"

I didn't know. It made sense that Sam would have been calling for us if it was him – but it didn't mean we would have heard him. The jungle was a big place, and we'd wandered a long way from our original entry point.

"But if it's an agent, why is he here?" I asked, pushing my matted hair back from my eyes and mopping sweat off my forehead with the back of a dirty hand.

"To capture us?" suggested my friend. He looked scared, and I knew he was also thinking they may be here to kill us, so I said: "If they meant us harm they wouldn't have bothered coming after us, would they? They'd have just left us to starve."

"But they don't know we've lost the DART," said Jake, and my stomach lurched. I hadn't thought of that. If they believed we could return home at any time, they may well have sent an agent after us, to make sure we didn't.

I stood up, stretched, and picked up my rucksack again. "In that case, hadn't we better get well away from the footprint, so we're as far away as possible from whoever it is?"

Jake stood up too, and Tin-o flapped his tiny wings in anticipation of yet another hike. We headed off into the jungle again, this time in the opposite direction from the muddy footprint.

That evening we slept up a tree, as usual, with Tin-o settling himself down in a patch of stubbly grass at the base.

We'd decided our pet dinosaur was a 'he' after debating for a while about how to sex a species we had no idea about – neither of us wanted to get too close to those claws and beak, however friendly it seemed. In the end we randomly assigned him the male gender, purely because both of us were male, and it didn't seem right we should be followed around by a female. Not before puberty, at any rate.

Tin-o seemed happy enough after we shared a tin

of baked beans with him – he didn't seem to be a fussy eater. He fluttered his wings, turned around several times and settled down with his tomato sauce-covered beak resting on his back.

Now we were full of beans, so to speak, we tried to make ourselves comfortable with ferns as our mattresses. We weren't really tired, but we had to get off the ground before the sun set as it was too dangerous otherwise.

The incessant insects, so annoying during the heat of the day, tended to die down during the night-time, and we could actually talk without having to wave our arms around in the air every two seconds to waft away a persistent fly.

As the sun set through the trees in another blaze of red and orange, Jake settled down in his bed of ferns, his rucksack tied to a branch with its straps so it wouldn't fall during the night.

I was dozing, watching the stars come out through a patch in the leaves above, wondering how many of them, too, were different from the ones in our universe. How many of those blazes of light had living beings circling them? The thought made me feel insignificant, small and a bit lonely.

"Do you know how big the universe is?" asked Jake suddenly, as if he'd been reading my mind. I shivered a little, and it wasn't just the gathering chill in the air.

"Er… no," I answered, thinking back to our Science classes last year with Mr Douglas. I couldn't remember discussing the size of the universe. Come to think of it, all I could remember was Adam Garner deliberately spilling acid on his desk, and Mr Douglas marching him off to the head. Douggie looked like he was going to explode, but Adam had a big grin on his face.

Jake stayed silent, so I went on: "Pretty big?"

My friend sighed the sigh he usually kept for when I was being particularly dim. "Well done, Einstein," he said, and I heard him shift his weight around. It was getting dark, and it went very dark really fast here. I could just about make out his shape.

"Well?" I asked. "You can't lead a person on with a question like that and not answer it. How big is the universe?"

"No-one really knows," he said dismissively, and if I had had something to throw at him I would have done so then. He must have heard me tutting, because he went on: "Well, we can measure the amount of time it must've taken for light from the farthest stars we can see to reach us – 14 billion years, I think, is the figure – and we know it takes light 100,000 years to cross the Milky Way, but that doesn't really tell us how big the universe is, because it could be just a part of something even bigger, or there could be other universes outside it, or…"

I stopped him. He wasn't exactly boring me, as such, but all this was not helping me feel less small than I'd been feeling a moment ago.

"Hang on," I said, "you and I know there are countless different universes, all existing at the same time, right?"

He seemed a bit put out to have been stopped mid-lecture, and I was glad I couldn't see his face. "Right," he said. I detected a sulk lurking in there.

"And you and I are, as far as we are aware, the only two schoolboys ever to have visited this dinosaur-ridden universe, right?"

"Dinoworld, right," said Jake, and I again cringed at the name.

"So I think we have every right to feel a bit special just now," I said, "however big the universe, stroke universes, is, stroke, are. Right?"

"Right," said Jake, still a little sulkily, and we fell silent. We were soon asleep.

I dreamt of home. Mum was baking cupcakes, and the smell was making me drool. Then Lizzie iced them, but instead of making a mess all over the kitchen and getting more of the icing on the worktops than on the cakes, as she usually did, she managed to form perfect pink peaks on each cake, which she topped off with a chocolate button on each one.

She brought me two of them on a tray, on a pretty

pink plate, alongside a steaming hot mug of tea and a bowl containing a huge piece of apple and blackcurrant crumble with hot custard dripping over the side.

"There you go, Ethan," she said, and she smiled sweetly up at me with her gappy smile. She'd lost another tooth, I saw. "You're the best brother in the world."

I patted her on the head, smiled, and reached out for the tray…

"Squark! Squark! Squark!"

My eyes flew open, and I saw it was pitch black. I could see nothing, though I heard Jake swearing under his breath a few feet away. Tin-o was squawking and flapping around at the foot of the tree, making enough noise to wake the dead. He was obviously rattled by something, but I was in no rush to find out what it was.

"Be quiet, you useless creature," said Jake – quite unfairly, I thought, as Tin-o was anything but useless. I shushed him. Whatever it was that was upsetting Tin-o, I didn't want it to know we were here. Jake went quiet, and all we could hear was our pet dinosaur as he flapped and fussed down below.

Suddenly the noise died away, and I concluded Tin-o had left the tree. It seemed our tin opener was deserting us – and I didn't want to think about how we'd eat now.

I also didn't want to think about what could be bad enough to make him leave his food supply. Unfortunately, I soon found out.

There was a commotion in the undergrowth below – a rustling of ferns and moving aside of shrubs. This was not uncommon at night – after all, the place was full of creatures, large and small, and some of them had to be nocturnal.

But so far when we'd heard animals at night we hadn't seen them, just been aware of their passing by, the big ones sounding like elephants, shaking the ground as they passed.

This time, though, was different. Frighteningly so.

This time, the creatures passing us on the ground below our tree could be seen, even in the pitch black night.

There were three of them. And they were carrying fire.

My first thought was a stupid one: But they can't have fire; Sam said they hadn't invented it yet. My second thought was almost as idiotic: Maybe it's Sam come to rescue us!

Of course it wasn't Sam. Sam would have an electric torch, not a fiery one – and he wouldn't be looking for us at night, would he? That would be ridiculous.

As the trio passed our tree, I caught a glimpse of a face lit by the flickering flames. It had big eyes – bigger than a human's – and a flattened nose, but that was all I saw before they disappeared off into the jungle.

And I heard them, speaking in a language I couldn't understand. They were talking to each other; hissing, growling words.

I waited, tense as a stretched elastic band, nerves jangling at every sound, waiting for them to return, but nothing did. Time passed, the night went quiet again, and I dared break the silence.

"What the hell were they?" I whispered.

Jake, from his perch on the other side of the tree, closer to where the creatures had passed us by, made a strangled kind of noise – in fright, I presumed, at hearing me speak. Then he said: "I saw them, Ethan. They were… they were…" My friend was lost for words, and I made a mental note, because that didn't happen very often.

"I only saw one of their faces," I said. "What could you see?"

He didn't speak for at least a minute, and I thought he hadn't heard me. I was about to ask him again, when he whispered: "There were three of them. They were walking on two legs, but I swear they had four arms each – one of them was carrying two torches, did you see?" He didn't wait for me to reply, but went on: "And they had clothes on – I couldn't see much, but they were definitely wearing something. Cloaks. But their faces, Ethan – they didn't look human."

"So what were they?" I asked.

My friend was silent again, and I thought he didn't have an answer to this one, but eventually his small voice interrupted the silence once more: "I think they were homo dinosaurians," he said.

"Ex-squeeze me?" I said, and I heard Jake laugh a little.

"Homo means man," said my friend, "and I think they're basically human-like beings evolved from dinosaurs. So, homo dinosaurian."

"But Sam never said anything about human dinosaurs!" I said, rather desperately, I have to admit.

"Well," said Jake, "Sam only spent a small amount of time in the dinosaur world he visited, because there was nothing of benefit there – and anyway, it's highly unlikely it's the same one. There must be thousands of universes where dinosaurs never became extinct. In some of them, presumably, the dinosaurs evolved into intelligent beings."

I thought about this for a while, realising I was both excited and terrified by the prospect, then said: "So was it one of them that made the footprint we saw today?"

Jake snorted laughter, then dissolved into a fit of giggles, which he was obviously trying to suppress. "What's so funny?" I asked, a little annoyed. "Ssh... they may hear us."

Jake got his laughter under control. "Sorry," he said. "It's just I doubt they've developed the same kind of training shoe as we have."

"They may have," I said, sulking.

Jake snorted again. "It had a Nike tick on the bottom," he said slowly, as if explaining something to a five-year-old.

"Did it?" I said, still sulking. "I didn't see that."

"It did," said Jake, "and I doubt the dinosaurs have the same sense of fashion as us humans."

"Oh," I said, and we went silent again. There didn't seem to be much else to say – the creatures, whatever they were, had gone, and we would have to wait until it was light before we decided what to do with this new knowledge; if anything. I mean, what could we do?

I don't think either of us slept much that night – we were both too much on edge. I did doze a little, but every time I slept I was haunted by nightmares about creatures with dead black eyes and grey faces, staring at me and prodding me with long fingers topped with claws.

....

In the morning I was woken from another nightmare – one I couldn't remember, thankfully – by Jake shaking me awake.

Instantly on edge again, I asked him what was the matter, but he just pointed to the ground. There was a smile on his face, which I thought was a bit odd in the circumstances.

I looked down, and managed a smile myself.

There, sitting with his legs under him and his beak on his scaly chest, lay Tin-o.

"Yay!" I said, as I stretched my legs and grabbed my rucksack, ready to climb down. "Breakfast!"

Jake was already down, talking to Tin-o like a long lost cat that has found its way home after two weeks missing.

"Where have you *been*?" he was saying, as I climbed down and stood next to him. "Did the nasty creatures scare you?"

I rolled my eyes. "He sees us as a source of food," I said, rubbing my back where it had gone stiff, "he's not a pet."

"I thought that's what most pets saw humans as," said Jake, opening his bag and taking out the few tins that remained. Tin-o was nosing inside the bag, and Jake shooed his beak away.

"What shall we have today then?" asked Jake. I wasn't sure who he was asking – me or the dinosaur – so I stayed silent. Jake didn't seem to mind. He chose a tin of ham, offered it to Tin-o, and watched as our friend expertly opened it.

"Thanks, mate," he said, as he picked up the two halves, scooped out a little ham with two fingers and threw it to the dinosaur as reward. He then gave me half a tin, which I ate using a small twig to prise out the meat. I ate standing up, I was so hungry.

After drinking some of our water, we decided to press on in the direction we'd been travelling yesterday – luckily, it was opposite to that in which the homo dinosaurians had gone during the night.

We didn't have a plan, of course. We'd given up looking for the DART, deeming it impossible, had no other way of getting back home apart from surrendering to the person with the Nike trainers (if we could find him; which of course was just as impossible), and now had these other intelligent creatures to look out for, as well as the ones planning on making a meal of us.

What else could we do except keep walking? Lie down and die? We'd wait until we had no food left before we thought about doing that. And even then I thought we may well just keep on walking until we dropped. It was what we did now.

We fought our way through thick jungle for some time until, hot and exhausted, dripping with sweat, we came upon another stream. We decided to rest in the shade for a while, after refilling our water bottles from the clear water.

Tin-o drank too, filling his red beak with water at the stream before tipping his head back and letting it trickle down his throat. The sun glinted off his feathers, and his useless little arms waved around in the air as usual – it looked like he was conducting an invisible orchestra.

"Why do you think he has arms that don't seem to do anything?" I asked.

Jake was sitting on the ground next to the stream, letting his fingers dangle in the water and occasionally dripping some onto his head. He looked at Tin-o, conducting his orchestra, shrugged, and said: "Maybe it's like a penguin's wings – they're left-overs from creatures they evolved from."

"But he's got useless wings, too," I said.

Jake nodded. "Yeah; have you noticed quite a few of the creatures we've come across have six limbs, not four; so his wings and arms are no longer needed as much, and they've shrunk. He only really needs his legs."

"And his beak," I said, as we watched him stab at a passing bug-like creature, black as night and as big as your hand, and eat it whole.

Jake made an 'I'm going to be sick' noise in his throat, and turned away. I wondered how long it would be before we, too, were reduced to catching and eating bugs, but said nothing.

After a rest we pressed on. As I said, there was little else to do.

An hour into our walk we noticed the vegetation thinning a little – clearings between the trees were longer, and we could walk easier, without having to push through shrubs and ferns so much. The atmosphere seemed fresher, too – less clammy.

And then, suddenly it seemed, we were on an open plain. The air was cooler, the sky seemed huge – I realised I could see the horizon for the first time.

Jake and I stood on the edge, stunned into silence. It really was beautiful. In the distance we could see purple mountains, but running between us and them were miles and miles of grassy, almost flat land. There were dinosaurs – 'proper' dinosaurs – in herds, grazing, but they were too far away to bother us just now. Wheeling around in the sky, again too far away to be a threat, were what seemed to be huge birds. I suddenly realised we hadn't seen any smaller ones, nor heard anything we would class as birdsong in the trees.

I breathed in the sweet fresh air. It seemed lighter, somehow, out of the oppression of the jungle.

"Race you to a brontosaurus," shouted Jake, and he ran off into the grassland. Tin-o followed, flapping and squawking happily.

I've never been a runner, as I think I've told you before, but I too was happy to run after them; besides, I didn't want to get left behind.

We bounded through long grass, leaping over odd clumps of flowers of all colours, laughing as we did so. I had no idea where we were going, but it didn't seem to matter. We were alive; we were free; it was beautiful.

I caught up with Jake quite easily – his legs aren't as long as mine – and we were running side-by-side, out of breath but still laughing, when the world fell out from under our feet.

There was a slipping, a scramble, a feeling of falling, and sudden and astonishing pain in my ankle as we crashed through what seemed to be a hole in the ground where moments before there had been no hole.

I looked up as we fell, saw the sky outlined far above us, saw fern leaves falling with us, and before I passed out had time to think that this wasn't a natural phenomenon.

This was a trap.

Trapped

I woke to pain. There was someone stabbing my ankle with a knife. The pain was shooting up my leg as far as my knee.

"Get off me!" I yelled, lashing out with my arms. But there was no-one there.

I opened my eyes. It was gloomy, but there was sun streaming in from above, lighting up the side of the hole we'd fallen into. The sides were made of smooth brown earth. I reckoned we were about twelve or fourteen feet down.

Jake was lying a few feet away on his back, his arms over his head and his legs at odd angles. He wasn't moving.

I immediately panicked, shuffled over to where he lay – my ankle was too badly hurt to stand on – and shook him. "Jake!" I said. "Wake up!"

Thankfully he started moving, and I knew he was

alright. Groaning, he untangled his limbs, sat up groggily, and looked at me, frightened.

"What happened?" he asked. I pointed upwards, to the sky above, and he nodded. "Oh," he said, and sighed. "Are you OK?"

I glanced at my right ankle, which looked alright but was hurting like hell. "I think I may have sprained my ankle," I said, "but otherwise yeah, I'm OK. You?"

Jake moved all his limbs in turn, then stood up. "I may never ballet dance again, but I think I'm in one piece," he said. He looked up at the sky, which now seemed a long way away. "I don't think we'll be able to climb out of here, though, which is another worry altogether."

I tried standing myself, felt stabbing pain again, and decided to stay where I was. My rucksack had come off in the fall, but was lying close by. Jake's was still on his back – it must have hurt to fall onto that, I thought.

Just then there was a squawking noise from above,

and Tin-o's red beak came into view over the lip of the hole. He was flapping his little wings and creating a fuss, hopping from leg to leg, obviously concerned his lunch was now unobtainable.

Jake looked up at him, craning his neck to see. "Go get us a ladder, there's a good boy," he shouted, flapping his hands like you do to shoo away an animal. Tin-o just squawked some more.

"Yeah, like that's going to work," I said.

Jake came and sat next to me. He took his rucksack from his back and put it on the ground. For a while we said nothing – what was there to say? We were in a hole, literally and metaphorically. Even standing on Jake's shoulders I wouldn't reach the top; and we had no rope or hope of rescue. Tin-o wasn't going to fetch help, was he?

After ten minutes Jake sprang to his feet, and started examining the sides of the hole. They were smooth and hard, like compacted sand speckled with harder, granite-like pieces of rock. He tried but couldn't make any impact on them with his fingers.

"How the hell did they dig this?" he asked.

I shuddered. "*Who* the hell dug this, more to the point," I said.

"Yeah, well I doubt it was the brontosauruses," said Jake.

"Brontosauri," I corrected.

"Really?" asked Jake. "Anyway, whoever it was had proper tools, and the intelligence to put those ferns on top to disguise the hole." He pointed at the floor, which was now strewn with fern leaves and small branches which presumably had been used to create a cover for the trap we'd fallen into. It had been a good disguise – we certainly hadn't seen it coming.

Tin-o was still squawking up above, and I suggested we get him to come down to us, so we at least had a tin opener for our remaining food. "Then we won't starve – well, at least not for a few days," I said, almost cheerily.

Jake looked at me as if I had gone mad. "You want that squawking, flapping, bad-tempered, tetchy, beaky thing down here?" he asked, amazed.

"Why not?" I asked.

"Well let me think…" said Jake in an exasperated tone. "What happens when we do run out of food, which is only a couple of days away?"

"Well…" I began, but Jake went on: "I'll tell you what will happen," he said. "Our dinosaur friend will get annoyed we no longer have food, and will turn his angry, stabby little beak and sharp claws on us. You've seen what he can do to a tin of beans – what do you think he'll do to your face?"

I pondered this for a while, before agreeing it was probably best to leave Tin-o where he was.

"You don't say," said Jake irritably, sitting down again, and getting out his water bottle. It was about half full, as was mine. So we'd probably die of dehydration before we starved. I decided not to tell Jake this; I was sure he knew it anyway.

"So what do we do now?" I asked at last.

My friend sighed. "We wait for whoever dug the hole to come and get us out," he said. He paused. "And hope they don't want to eat us when they do."

....

In the end we were only down the hole a day, although it seemed like eternity.

Tin-o had long since given up and gone away, presumably to catch some food of his own. It was quiet without him.

We rationed our water to a couple of sips an hour, but it still seemed to be going really fast, and we ate every last crumb of food we could find in our rucksacks – that not in tins, of course – until all that was left was a pack of dry noodles and the packet of hated apricots.

We decided to leave them until the morning.

That night we slept on a bed of fern leaves, gathered from around the floor of the hole. There weren't a lot, and the ground was hard, but we were too exhausted to mind. We slept, the total darkness around us; waking every now and then to the noise of animals up above, stamping and calling in their strange languages.

In the morning we woke at dawn, the thin light steeping in from the hole above. It seemed grey and forbidding, and I was cold for the first time since we'd arrived in this universe.

Jake saw me shivering and offered me his spare jumper. I thanked him, and put it on under my hoodie. We sat, nibbling at the dried apricots as if they were a delicacy neither of us had tasted before.

"These are actually quite nice," said Jake, through a mouthful of fruit.

"That's only because we've been living on nothing but Spam and hot dogs for days," I said, taking a second one. "Even dates would taste nice at this rate." There were only about twelve in the pack, so we limited ourselves to two each for breakfast.

I flexed my ankle. It didn't hurt as much as yesterday, but I still couldn't stand on it without collapsing. Jake, too, was full of aches – he reckoned he was bruised all over from the fall.

"Do you think they expect animals to die when they fall down here, so they don't have to kill them afterwards?" asked Jake. I did wish he wouldn't keep coming up with such cheery thoughts.

"I expect so," I said gloomily. "I wouldn't want to have to hunt any of the creatures we've seen so far, would you? They're all quite vicious. And bitey. So I expect they leave traps to catch food as an alternative to hunting."

Jake then had another upsetting thought: "If that's the case, maybe they only check the traps every week or so – so any animals caught in them will have starved to death if they weren't killed by the fall."

"Oh great." I said. "That's cheered me right up."

"Sorry," said my friend, and he went to check on our water bottles for the fifth time that morning. He was holding one up when he suggested we start urinating into the bottles, in order to conserve what liquid we had.

I nearly choked on the last mouthful of my apricot. "You've got to be kidding," I said.

He didn't sound like he was kidding. "It's a basic survival technique, when your water supply is limited," he added.

I grimaced. "Well you do what you like, it's your water," I said, and grabbed my own bottle closer. "But you're not peeing in mine."

"You'll wish you had when you're down to your last few sips," Jake said, unscrewing the top and peering inside.

"No… no, really, I won't," I replied.

"Suit yourself," said Jake, and, to my relief, he screwed the top back on and came and sat down.

We spent the morning alternately dozing and chatting; remembering the good times we'd had in what we were already seeing as our 'other life.' We laughed at memories of playing pranks on the teachers last term, and cried a little over how much we missed our families. I really thought I'd never see mum, Sam and Lizzie again.

At one point a beetle-like creature, as big as my hand, fell into the hole from above. It landed in the middle of the floor on its back, with a thud, its six legs wiggling uselessly in the air.

I yelled, surprised. I'd never liked insects back home, and those here were huge and scary-looking, so I cowered away to the side of the hole. But Jake went over to it, pushed it upright with his foot, and stood back as it got its bearings.

It had four antennae, each as long as my little finger, which it wiggled in the air. Each antenna had a blob at the end, like an eye. It was a uniform dark green colour, but not a shiny green; a murky, dull green.

After eyeing us up for a minute it scuttled off under a pile of fern leaves pushed up to one side of the hole. I shuddered again, and reminded myself not to sleep over there that night.

That afternoon we moved from one side of the hole to the other to avoid the sun, which was hot and burning down here with no breeze to lessen its effects. I took off Jake's jumper, and we ate a couple more apricots – we were already finding them horrible again, but there was nothing else to eat – and took a few sips of water before lying down in what little shade there was to rest.

We said little. I kept looking up above to see if anyone/thing was there, half dreading, half hoping. Midway through the afternoon I was watching a few wispy clouds blowing across the bright blue sky when I realised something else had moved into my field of vision.

It was a face. A long, grey face with large black, oval-shaped eyes, a squashed nose and a wide mouth with thin lips.

They'd come for us.

Out of the frying pan…

I stood up, jolting my ankle as I did so but not really noticing. "Jake!" I cried. My heart was beating hard in my chest – I don't think I've ever been so terrified before.

Jake glanced up from where he'd been lying, saw me looking upwards and followed my gaze. He quickly got to his feet. His face was white as a sheet. We looked at each other, then back to the top of our hole. The face was gone.

For a moment I thought I may have imagined it – after all, I had been half asleep – but then Jake said, in a small and scared voice: "I think he's gone to get reinforcements."

I looked around for my weapon, such as it was, but couldn't remember where I'd put it. Come to think of it, I wasn't even sure it was down here. Anyway, what use would a boy and a stick be against the kind of creatures who could create a sophisticated trap like this one?

Jake had the same idea about defence, and his club was close by, so he picked it up. I just shrugged. "I think I've lost mine," I said.

We waited, standing ready, for around ten minutes. It seemed like forever. Sweat was running down my back and my heart was still thudding behind my ribs. I could hear Jake's quick breathing.

Suddenly there was a commotion up above, and five, no, six, grey faces appeared around the rim. They were peering down at us, chattering to each other in strange guttural, hissing noises.

"I think they're deciding what to do with us," said Jake, before shouting up at them: "Hey you! Get us out! We're friends!"

I almost smiled at his optimism. "I don't think they understand English," I said, but he ignored me and went on anyway: "Yes, we can talk! See, we're intelligent beings, just like you! Come and get us out and we can show you all sorts of things!"

"Yeah, we've got noodles and a bandage!" I said,

under my breath.

"We have food, see?" shouted Jake, picking up the packet of apricots and waving it in the air above his head.

I nearly laughed. I think I was mildly hysterical. "We'll exchange them for a leg of stegosaurus, if that helps," I said. Jake threw me a withering look, then turned to me. "If they see us as something more interesting than food, they may treat us well," he said, angrily. "Stop messing about and act confidently; they may recognise us as superior beings."

I raised one eyebrow. "What are you, a Nazi? Who said we're superior?" I said, but Jake was continuing with his plan. I grudgingly admitted to myself it was better than mine; mainly because I didn't have one.

The creatures up above were obviously having an argument about what we were and what to do with us; they were pointing with long fingers and gabbling in their odd language. I had time to wonder how I would react to finding a totally alien being in a trap I had set

– I'd be scared, certainly, but also curious and intrigued – before they acted.

Quick as a flash, with no warning, two of them jumped down into the hole – it was small, so no more than two of them would fit. Surprised at their actions – no human could've jumped that far with such confidence and speed – Jake and I were unable to act; before we could even get a proper look at our new companions, we found ourselves covered by something heavy and ropey. The homo dinosaurians had thrown a type of net over our heads, to contain us and disarm us, I suppose. I felt rough hands and arms encircling my body, grabbing at my own arms and pinning them to my sides, before I was tripped up and landed heavily on the floor. A heavy weight fell on top of me.

In less than a minute both Jake and I were trussed up like turkeys, unable to move, our legs and arms tied together with a type of prickly, rough rope, our heads and shoulders covered with the nets. Although there were holes in the net, I couldn't see anything, and was finding it difficult to breathe until the creature got off me and roughly pulled me upright.

Then something else was tied tightly to my waist – I could feel the creature's claws digging into my side as it attached another rope – and I found myself being hoisted up from above, the creature holding me tightly with thin but strong arms. I couldn't see much, but I presume the homo dinosaurians were sort of abseiling up the sides of the holes, taking us with them, dangling on the end of ropes pulled from above.

It was a rough and painful journey, but thankfully short. By the time we got to the top I had been bashed against the rocky sides, the ropes were digging into my wrists and ankles, and the one round my waist felt like it had cut a groove all the way to my kidneys.

I could hear Jake struggling and swearing a few feet away, but couldn't see anything because the net was in front of my eyes.

Unable to move, I was picked up by at least six hands, hoisted into a lying-down position, face to the sky, and carried like a roast pig. The comparison frightened me. At this point, bruised, battered and tied up, I fully expected to be tossed into a cauldron of boiling water and made into a stew.

Although I don't believe in any god – I've been an atheist since I stopped believing in Father Christmas – I admit I was praying as the alien beings carried me to an unknown fate. Not to any recognisable superior being, you understand; rather to anyone, anywhere – it was the 'please let me get out of this alive; I'll be really good from now on' type of bargaining prayer we human beings resort to in a crisis.

I was carried like a piece of meat for quite some time; I can't tell you how long, but I was beginning to fall asleep, lulled by the motion, when they finally put me down.

I was placed quite gently on the floor, on my back, so again I couldn't see anything other than the sky and some trees. Unable to move my head to look around, I didn't even know if Jake was there too. I could hear the creatures talking. I groaned, scared and in pain, and tried to kick out with my legs, but nothing would move.

I felt myself being poked and prodded – by what I don't know – and tried to shout out, but the net was against my mouth and I couldn't really move it. I decided to just lie still – well, there was very little else I could do.

After a short time the net was removed from over my head, and I felt immediate relief. I could breathe properly, and could see and hear more of what was going on. I looked about for Jake, and was pleased to see him about four feet away, propped up against a tree. A creature was taking the net off his head, and I got my first proper look at this weird species.

The homo dinosaurians were taller than us – I'd say no less than six and a half feet – and thin, with long legs and four arms; the second pair of arms started at their waists, but their bodies were straighter than ours, and they didn't seem to have any hips. Their arms were long, too, ending in thin, bony hands with six fingers on each, two of which were smaller and seemed to serve as thumbs, one at each end.

Every brittle-looking finger ended in a long, curving claw, but their feet didn't have claws – the six toes were rounded at the end, more like split hooves. They were barefoot.

Their faces were long and thin, too, with features generally human-like, and in the same position, but elongated and exaggerated. The eyes were large and always black, with huge pupils and long eyelashes like a camel's; the nose was stubby and squashed, but had two nostrils, like ours, and the mouth was wide, with no lips. When they opened their mouths you could see many small, sharp teeth and a long and thin tongue, like a lizard's. I couldn't see any ears. Their skin was uniformly the same colour – a greenish grey – and looked rough and a bit scaly. They had no hair, but a couple had a few dull green feathers on the back of their heads. Most were bald, their heads more oval-shaped than ours.

They all seemed to be wearing the same basic clothing – a long thin cloak, always green, tied around their necks with a thin rope. I didn't get a close look, so I don't know what it was made of – I presume some sort of animal skin. Apart from this they were naked, but they didn't seem to have any… ahem… private parts. They were as smooth 'down there' as a Ken doll. There was no way of knowing if they were male or female – I don't even know if they had different sexes; they all looked alike.

Jake and I stared at each other in a despairing way. He looked tired and hurt – I could see he was bleeding from a small cut on his right cheek. "You OK?" I asked.

Before he could answer, one of the creatures came and stood in-between us, looking at Jake. It crouched down on its knees, like we do, and waved its four arms around in the air, hissing and growling in its weird language.

Jake assumed it was trying to communicate with him, so started explaining who we were and where we'd come from. I thought this was a waste of time, to be honest, and I was right; less than two sentences in (Jake had got to: "We're from a parallel universe") the creature waved three of its arms, hissed once more and left.

I looked around, as best I could from my lying-down position. We were in a clearing back in the jungle we had so recently left. The six creatures who had taken us out of the hole were to one side, sitting on the ground in a circle, legs crossed, talking and occasionally glancing in our direction. One of them kept gesturing with a clawed hand towards Jake. It was obvious they were discussing what to do with us. I just hoped it didn't involve dinner.

I turned my head to look at Jake. Blood was trickling into his mouth, and he was spitting it away.

"What do you think they're going to do with us?" I asked. My voice came out all thin and squeaky, so I cleared my throat. I may have been scared, but I didn't want to sound it.

Jake sighed. "I doubt they'll be inviting us home to meet their mothers," he said.

We lay there, tied up and unmoving, hot, aching, hungry and thirsty, until dusk, at which point two of our captors got up, disappeared into the jungle and came back five minutes later with four blazing torches. How they lit them we didn't see.

The remaining four got up too, came over to where we lay and picked us up, hoisting us onto their shoulders with their four arms.

The two torch-bearing creatures walking in front to light the way, the four carried Jake and I further on into the thick jungle.

Maybe we were going to meet the relatives after all.

…into the fire

That journey – being carried aloft by two alien creatures, tied up, aching all over, very thirsty and nearly starving – was probably the worst I've ever had.

The uncertainty of where we were going and what would happen to us when we got there was almost overwhelming. My stomach felt like a washing machine, churning away with worry, and if I had eaten anything other than a few apricots in the last day or so I felt sure it would all be coming back up again sometime soon.

It was rapidly getting dark, and I could see nothing apart from odd glimpses of the darkening sky above, in-between the dense trees. Everything seemed to be aching – my legs, my side, my arms, but especially my wrists, which had been tied together too tightly. The harsh rope was digging into them, and for a while I concentrated on this pain as a way of forgetting everything else.

Eventually – it must have been at least an hour later, but of course I had no way of knowing – I noticed the trees thinning out, and the sky above us broadened into a huge expanse of endless, countless stars. I'd never seen so many, and even in my terror I was aware of being awestruck at the magnificence and vastness of the universe.

But my awe was soon turned into fright again when the creatures carrying me suddenly stopped and placed me unceremoniously on the floor, like they were dropping a heavy bag. The ground was hard, and I'm sure I gained a few more bruises from the drop-off.

I heard Jake say "Ouch! Don't be so rough!" as he, too, was deposited on the ground, and I almost laughed. I think it may have been hysteria again, but it was also partly relief that my friend was still with me.

I turned to look in his direction, but could barely make him out. It was very dark, with the only light coming from the creatures' flaming torches, which had burnt down considerably, I saw.

One of the dinosaurians stayed with us, a torch in hand, while the other five strode off and disappeared into the darkness.

I turned my head to look at him/her, standing a few feet away. This one had something strapped to its waist, as well as the obligatory cloak over its shoulders. Made of the same green material, it resembled a bag and was bulging out, as if it was full. It looked heavy. I presumed they had tools and food, just like we did, and had to carry them around somehow.

I was about to ask Jake if he was OK – I knew it was pointless, but hey, that's what you do, isn't it? – when my friend started talking to the creature again.

"Excuse me, do you think I could have some water? I'm really thirsty."

I did laugh this time. "Can we have a three course meal, too, please? We're starving!" I called. Jake told me to shut up. The creature just looked at us blankly. Of course it had no idea what we were saying.

"Maybe they don't even drink themselves," I said

to Jake. "I mean, have you seen them eating or drinking yet? And we've been with them for hours now."

Jake sighed. "I suppose it's possible," he said. "They could be related to lizards – they look a bit lizardy – so maybe they don't need much water. Maybe they get all their moisture from their food."

"Well I'm not very moist right now," I replied, and it was Jake's turn to laugh. "I don't think they'll eat us," he said, although I had no idea how he came to this conclusion, and wasn't going to ask.

We stayed silent for a while, the only sounds the usual jungle animal noises, which we were used to by now. Alone with my thoughts, they started to wander back home, to mum, Lizzie and Sam, and I have to admit I started crying a little. They all seemed so far away now.

I was just remembering how mum used to tell me a story at night when I was little, and how I'd make her read a dinosaur book I had over and over – how ironic, I thought now – when there was a noise as the dinosaurians who had left us some time ago returned.

They gestured towards us, spoke to the one who had stayed, and then hoisted us up again.

"Oh not again!" I heard Jake moan. "Can't you lot settle down?"

This time, though, the journey was only short. After another five minutes of being carried the creatures put us down yet again, this time propping us up with our backs against something solid, and I looked around in amazement.

They'd taken us to meet the relatives, alright.

We were now in a large clearing, with the odd tree dotted around but otherwise clear of plants. Facing us were five or six large, low mud huts, with circular holes as windows and intricately woven fern leaves as roofs. They had narrow door-holes which were covered with the same leaves, bonded together somehow to serve as doors. From each hut window a flickering light could be seen, and I gathered inside was lit with torches or some kind of firelight.

Outside there were clear pathways between each hut, and on these pathways rows of flaming torches were placed on three-foot-tall wooden pillars, to light the way. The pathways and accompanying lights disappeared into the darkness on all sides, and I got the impression the village was bigger than just the huts we could see at the moment.

"I think they've brought us to their leader," said Jake in a quiet, awed voice. I nodded, though I don't know if he saw me or not. I was too awestruck myself to talk.

A thought occurred to me, and I turned my head to see what we were leaning against. It was another hut, but this time smaller, and I couldn't see any windows or doors. It was obviously made out of earth – the term mud hut was accurate, then – which had been made smooth by many hands. I could see lines and even the odd palm-print left by the creatures' scaly hands on the wall between Jake and I.

Three of the dinosaurians had left, while the remaining three were huddled together a few feet away, talking quietly in their strange hissing voices. One of them kept turning its head to look at us, and I got the impression it was uneasy about something.

I was just thinking it was odd no-one from the village had come out to look at us, when the three who had gone away returned with two more in tow. One of them was wearing a red cloak – everyone else's was green – and had distinct red feathers on its head, and when it approached us the three who had stayed suddenly dropped to the floor, all four hands upraised as if they were afraid.

"And I think that's him," mumbled Jake, as the red-feathered one approached us warily. It stood looking at us, talking to the others in a harsh, grunting way. The three on their knees got up and came and stood by us, pointing with their claws, and chattering in what sounded like an excited manner. This discussion went on for some time, and after a while Jake decided to interrupt.

"Er, hello," he said, in a clear, loud voice. "We're pleased to meet you… er, Sir. My name's Jake, and this is Ethan. We're from another…" But he was totally ignored by our hosts, who just glanced at him before continuing their dialogue.

"Don't waste your breath," I said. "I suppose it's like us listening to a pig squealing. It means nothing to them." Jake sighed. He was doing a lot of sighing lately, and I wasn't sure I could blame him.

The creatures continued debating for some time, and frankly I was getting bored of being treated like a piece of meat, when four of them came over, grabbed us by the arms and pulled us to our feet. Our wrists and ankles were still tied together, remember, so we couldn't walk, but they lifted us – two each – and took us around the corner to the back of the hut we'd been leaning against. There was a doorway there – this one with no door – and they took us inside, before laying us down once more, this time on our backs. Then they left us alone.

The hut was quite small, from what we could gather while only being able to look at the ceiling, and was in darkness. There was no cheery fire or torch-light in here, just a cold, hard earth floor and a leafy roof. There were no windows. Aside from a small amount of firelight creeping in from the open doorway, it was dark.

"Oh great," breathed Jake, and I thought he may have been crying. "We're really screwed now." I was too frightened to say anything.

A few minutes later I trusted myself to speak again. "Why do you think they put us in here?" I asked quietly. My wrists were sore, I was really thirsty and I wanted nothing more than to be at home in bed. I'd never missed home so much in my life.

Jake laughed a little. It was not a good sound. "I suppose they have no idea what we are, or what to do with us," he said. "They're probably going to sleep on the problem. I expect the leader will come and visit us again in the morning. Maybe they'll put our fate to the vote."

I wriggled my hands against their constraints again, but the rope was too tight to even move. "Are your ropes loose enough to get free?" I asked. "Mine aren't."

"No," said Jake at once. "Don't you think I've

tried already? They're done up tighter than a… than a… oh I can't even think of anything…" He sounded so sad I thought I was going to cry, but blinked the tears away. They wouldn't help.

A couple of minutes went by, while both of us tried struggling against the ropes. It was pointless; they were really strong.

"They've got a guard on the door, anyway," said Jake in an exasperated tone. "So even if we did get free we'd have to get past him." I turned my head to look at the doorway, but I could only see a shadow. Jake's eyesight was obviously better than mine.

"But they don't seem to have any weapons," I said, "so we could probably just push our way past. Or wait until he falls asleep?"

"Well, it's a waste of time thinking that," said my friend. "We can't get out of these ropes, and we can't escape tied up. And even if we could, we don't have our rucksacks anymore. We haven't even got water bottles, let alone food."

"No," I said, and lay back, exhausted. We hadn't

had any food or drink for ages, and I was beginning to feel really weak. I thought we may just have to admit defeat, and wait and see what tomorrow brought. Maybe we could somehow show the creatures that we needed feeding – or maybe they'd realise it themselves.

Yeah, and maybe pigs would fly, I thought. To them we were strange animals… and it didn't look like they were much into animal rights.

I lay back and closed my eyes. Man, I was tired. I didn't expect to fall asleep so easily, but soon I was dreaming.

………………………………………………

Someone was shaking me by the shoulder.

"Wake up." It was a loud whisper, in my ear, but it wasn't Jake's voice. It was a man's.

My eyes flew open. It was still pitch black, and I could see nothing. I was about to shout out, when a large, rough hand was put over my mouth to stop me.

“Be quiet. If you want to go home, don’t speak. In order to DART you have to be awake.”

My eyes opened wider than ever, and my heart started thudding in my chest. It was so loud I thought the creatures outside might hear it.

The voice continued in its whisper: “I’m going to wake your friend up now, and I want you to stay still and quiet. Can you do that?” I nodded, and the man removed his hand from my mouth.

I heard him go over to Jake and repeat the waking up process. Jake squeaked a little, but was remarkably quiet otherwise. The man returned to me, and I heard him again: “Shuffle over this way – we need to be close to DART successfully. Just a little more… OK, let’s leave this hellhole.”

He grabbed my arm with a firm grasp, and the next thing I knew light was flooding in, my eyes hurt, there was a cold hard floor under my body, I could see a fluorescent light on a white tiled ceiling, and…

And there was mum, sitting on a chair in front of me, Lizzie on her knee, Sam standing by their side.

We were home. Somehow, we had made it home.

Safe at last

Mum leapt up from the chair, almost throwing Lizzie to the floor in her excitement and haste.

"Ethan! Ethan! Oh my God, thank God! Ethan!" She dropped to the ground, where Jake and I still lay trussed up like Christmas turkeys, and grabbed me around the shoulders, raising me from the cold, un-carpeted floor in a giant bear hug. I could barely breathe.

"Thank God! Thank God you're safe!" She was crying – man, I was crying too, I'm not ashamed to admit – and laughing at the same time.

"Thank God!" It seemed to be all she could say, but then she released me and held me at arms' length to look at me properly. There were tears rolling down her cheeks.

"Mum!" I said through my tears, equally lost for words.

Sam broke the madness by interrupting: "Can you

please untie the boys, Johnny, so we can have a proper reunion?"

The man who'd brought us home – Johnny, I presumed – was already cutting Jake's ropes with a sharp 6-inch-long knife. It took some sawing to get Jake free, then he cut mine. I rubbed both my wrists in turn and looked briefly at them – they were red raw – before turning back to mum and hugging her. A hug had never felt so good before.

Next was Lizzie's turn. She was crying too much to speak, bless her, but gave me a huge hug while mum moved on to Jake ("Jake! Thank God! Jake!")

"Oh Lizzie I missed you!" I said through my tears, and she wailed even louder.

I looked over to Jake, and saw he was grinning like an idiot. His hair was filthy, his face was red, sunburnt and covered in mud and blood, he was skinny as a rake, his clothes were torn and dirty and he stank like a racehorse when it's just finished the Grand National, but he was grinning like he'd just won the Lottery. In a way we had.

After hugging Sam too (he spared me the Thank Gods, but there were still tears in his eyes), I turned to thank our saviour, Johnny.

A large, muscular man, I recognised him at once as one of the I-ART agents who had been coming for us in the barn. At first this scared me a little, but then I realised he had saved us, and, once I had rubbed some feeling back into my ankles, I stood up and staggered a little over to where he was now standing at the side of the small room, watching the reunion. The room was a bare one, I saw, with no furniture in it apart from the plastic chair mum had been sitting in. There were no windows.

Dressed all in black, our new friend looked like a soldier, with two large knives and a handgun strapped to his belt along with other equipment I couldn't identify. He had short blond hair and piercing blue eyes, and was smiling. He too looked a bit grubby, but otherwise very professional and tidy.

I was going to thank him, but he spoke first. "Well, lad," he said, "you two certainly led me on a wild goose chase back there. Do you know I was trying to find you for days?"

I thought back to the footprint we'd seen, glanced down at his black army boots – there was a Nike tick on the side – and said: "Sorry… we didn't know you were trying to help us."

"That's OK, lad," said the man. "It must have been terrifying for you. Good job I came across you when I did. I was beginning to run out of food and would have had to come back soon." And abandon us to our uncertain fate, presumably.

The mention of food made my stomach rumble loudly, and mum obviously heard it. "They need feeding," she said abruptly. She was standing behind me, gazing at me as if she hadn't seen me before. "Everything else can wait until later. You must be starving."

Jake muttered something about not having eaten for ten days – I wasn't even sure we'd been away that long, but never mind – and mum ushered us towards the door.

There I was surprised to see another two uniformed men, apparently on guard outside the room, open the door with a key. We'd been locked in.

I was about to ask why, and where we were, and a whole lot of other questions which suddenly occurred to me, when Sam put his hand on my shoulder. I thought he must have read my mind. "We can talk later, Ethan. Right now you and Jake need a wash, clean clothes, some food and drink and a rest. The people here will look after you well."

"Don't worry," he added, as I opened my mouth to say something, "you can trust them." I looked at his face, and although he was smiling – and despite his reassuring words – he looked worried.

....

An hour later Jake and I had showered – I enjoyed the longest, hottest shower I have ever had, and used up so much soap I thought someone would complain – and were dressed in clean clothes. The clothes were our own, but we didn't bother to ask where they'd come from. It just felt so nice to put clean, dry clothes on again.

When we were dressed, a woman we didn't know showed us into a cosy room with a dining table and four chairs, a red carpet on the floor and bookshelves lining the walls. There were no windows again.

The woman, who was also dressed in a black uniform, and had her red hair up in a huge bun on top of her head, asked us if we liked chicken. Jake answered: "Hell, we'd eat dinosaur right now, if you happen to have any!" and the woman smiled, before leaving and returning a few minutes later with a small plate of plain chicken, rice and mixed vegetables each.

We'd already had a small drink of water, before we showered, but she placed a large jug of water on the table next to two glasses. "Don't drink too much," she said. "You're not used to it, and it will make you ill. Try and sip. And don't eat too fast, either. Your stomachs will have shrunk, and you'll feel sick if you do."

"Yes, mum," I said, before picking up the small piece of chicken in my fingers and eating it in almost one bite. The woman tutted and left the room. I swear I heard a key turn in the lock, but was too hungry to care.

Jake was already forking rice into his mouth at an alarming rate, and I laughed in-between mouthfuls of veg. "Slow down, Jake, you'll throw it all back again in a minute," I said.

He grinned at me through his food. "I've never been so ravenous for carrots and peas before," he spluttered.

"I didn't think you liked peas," I said with a mouthful of rice. "I don't!" he laughed, and we finished our meal in silence. It didn't take long.

Afterwards we sat with glasses of water cradled in our hands as if they were hot chocolate – oh, hot chocolate; I decided I was going to ask for one of those later – and tried not to feel ill. "What's for pudding?" I asked, and Jake groaned. It is amazing how little food you actually need, once you get used to eating less.

I looked around the room. The bookshelves were neatly stocked, and I read a few of the titles out of boredom. “The Causes of the Second Rebellion,” “Life and Death in the 19th Century,” “Guns, Guts and Gargoyles – a Soldier’s Tale,” and then my heart stopped when I got to the next one.

“Jake,” I said shortly.

“Yeah?”

“Somehow I don’t think we’re home, after all.” My throat was suddenly dry again, despite the water.

“What do you mean? Of course we’re home. I was going to ask them if I could ring mum and dad later. They’ll be so worried. God knows where they think I’ve been.”

I went over to the bookshelf and picked the book out by its spine. I turned it over to see the back, read what was printed on it, then handed it to Jake.

“What?” he said, bemused and looking worried by now.

“What does it say?” I asked.

Jake looked down at the book. "Parallel Universes: Basic Theory… yeah, so what? We have parallel universe theory in our world."

You know, for someone so intelligent he was being a bit dense. "Look at the back," I said.

Jake turned the book over and read out loud: "Since 1979, when scientists first discovered that parallel universes exist and Garner and Unsworth made their breakthrough in molecular transference… oh… right." Jake put the book on the table and stared at it blankly.

"Yeah," I said. "We're not home at all. I think we're in Sam's universe."

Prisoners

We read some of the other book titles, but none of them seemed to give us any clues as to where we were. Most of them were about soldiers and wars.

"What does it mean?" I asked Jake. He was standing up now, pacing round the room worriedly.

"It means the agents took us all back to their universe, of course," he said, adding: "We should have realised; they had come to capture Sam, not to rescue us."

"What do you think they're going to do with us?" I asked next. I knew Jake had no more idea than I did, but he was supposed to be the intelligent one; maybe he'd have some inkling.

Jake stopped pacing the windowless room and sat down again, before suddenly getting up and going to the door. He pulled on the door handle, but it didn't open. It was locked, alright.

"They've locked us in," he said, pointlessly. "That

means we're prisoners."

I nodded, sad now. If we were prisoners, that meant Sam was in danger of being put on trial for deserting the agency. And if he went on trial, he had already told us he could face the death penalty for his actions. My stomach lurched, and I thought I might bring back the dinner I had so recently enjoyed.

"I feel sick," I said. Jake sat down opposite me, and stared at the windowless wall.

"Well, at least we're together," he said. "And I-ART did send someone to rescue us from the dinosaurs; they can't be all that bad."

I looked at him and tried to smile. "Yeah," I said. "They did save us from Dinoworld, didn't they?"

Jake positively grinned as I used his name for the universe we'd been in. "Dinoworld, yeah," he said. "I think when we get back home I'm going to write everything that happened there down, you know, for posterity."

"For your grandchildren to read," I laughed.

"Yeah," he repeated. Then he looked sad again.

"What's the matter?" I asked.

"I'm worried about mum and dad," he said. "Do you think they'll be OK?"

I imagined Jake's family – he had an older brother and sister, too – back home in our reality, where he had now been missing for… what? I tried to count up how long we'd been gone, and couldn't. I'd lost track of days.

"How long have we been away?" he asked, reading my mind as usual.

"I don't know," I said slowly, trying to think. "We ran away from home on the Tuesday of half-term, and we were in the barn for… five days?" I looked at Jake, and he nodded agreement. "So that takes us to the Sunday," I said, counting the days on my fingers. "We should have been back to school on the Monday, but instead we were in Dinoworld, and we were there for… hell, I don't know; it felt like forever."

"I think it was about five days again," said my friend, his eyes widening, "which means we've been 'missing' for more than a week. Oh my… mum will be frantic." He went quiet, and I thought how lucky I was, at least, that my family was with me and not sat at home wondering where I had gone.

Just then the door opened, and in walked the woman with the bun who had given us dinner earlier. She cleared up the plates, saying nothing, not even when we started asking her questions. She smiled briefly, said we'd be seen to soon, and left, locking the door behind her.

I sighed. I almost missed the freedom of Dinoworld for a second, then remembered how hot and hungry we had been.

We sat there for what seemed like hours, Jake picking through some of the books on the shelf, but not being able to concentrate on reading, me just sitting, staring blankly and worrying. I started to bite my nails.

After a while – we had no idea what time it was; there was no clock in the room – someone opened the door and came in. It was Johnny, the agent who had rescued us from the dinosaur world. He looked cleaner and fresher and I assumed he, too, had showered and eaten.

He smiled at us, and came and sat down on one of the chairs.

We both started asking him tons of questions at the same time, and he held up a hand to silence us.

"Woah there, boys, just hold your horses," he said. We shut up. "That's better. I just came to say goodbye, as I'm going off duty. And I wanted to check you were OK before I left."

I opened my mouth to ask a question, but he interrupted me: "You'll see your family very soon. They're very anxious to see you, too. And I'm sure they'll answer all your questions."

Jake butted in: "But my family is in our universe. They'll think I've been abducted, or murdered, or something. I've not spoken to them since half term! Can't you let me go home?"

The agent was shaking his head. "I'm afraid we can't do that, Jake," he said. My friend started to protest, saying something about the Geneva Convention and the Bill of Human Rights, but Johnny put up his hand again. It was a big hand, and one you didn't want to argue with, so Jake went quiet.

"You can't go home until after the trial," said Johnny.

"Trial? What trial?" I asked, knowing the answer but hoping he meant something else. Johnny turned to me. "Samuel's trial," he said, "for desertion." My heart sank.

He went on: "You're both witnesses, and may be called to give evidence, so you have to be here until it's all over. But don't worry, Jake, I've been assured your parents have been made aware that you are safe."

"How?" asked my friend. "You can't exactly tell them where I am, can you? Or where I've been?"

"Of course not," said the agent, smiling. "That would cause a bit of bother we could do without. I don't know the details; they just said to let you know it was OK."

Jake didn't look very convinced, and neither was I. How could you explain him being away from home and school for so long with no contact? They'd surely have reported him as missing by now, which meant, when we did get back home, there'd be a lot of explaining to do. I wasn't looking forward to that.

Still, we were just kids, there was nothing we could do about it, so we had to concentrate on the here and now. Sam's trial, for instance.

"When will the trial be?" I asked, anxious that we may be here for some time. I mean, back home I knew cases could take years before they reach a courtroom.

Johnny shrugged his large shoulders. "I'm not sure," he said. "Usually it would take months…" I gasped, and he went on: "but in this case, because we're detaining people from another universe, I think they'll speed it up, so you can get back home as soon as possible."

"So we are prisoners, then?" asked Jake. He was fiddling with a book he had been reading, picking at its cover nervously.

Our new friend smiled. "Well, they won't let you leave," he said, "but technically you're witnesses, not prisoners."

"And what if I demand to be taken home?" asked Jake. There was a shake in his voice, and I knew he wasn't really serious about the demanding.

Johnny smiled again. There was nothing bad in that smile, but it wasn't very cheering. "They won't do that, I'm afraid. Not until the trial is over." Jake sighed loudly, and I felt sorry for him.

"Anyway," he went on, "don't you want to help your friend? He could be in serious trouble."

My ears pricked up, and I asked: "Do you mean if he's found guilty?"

Johnny nodded, looking serious now. "From what I understand you boys are going to be called to give evidence for the defence; that's why you're being kept separate from Sam and your family, Ethan – you're not allowed to talk to Sam without someone being there, in case he tells you what to say."

"Evidence for the defence?" said Jake. "What evidence?"

"Well," said the man, "I don't know, but I think

they'll call you as character witnesses; to prove Sam's actions since he deserted… I mean, left… were with good intentions." "Of course they were!" I interrupted. "Sam's a really nice man!"

Johnny smiled again. "I know they're gathering other character witnesses, too," he said, "so I think he's got a good chance of escaping."

"Escaping?" asked Jake.

Our new friend looked embarrassed. "Well…" he stuttered, "I mean, I'm sure he'll get away with it; they're not as harsh with deserters as they used to be…" he trailed off, but I pressed him: "Escaping from what?" I asked, though I feared I already knew the answer.

Johnny's face twisted as he tried to think of a good way of putting it, and failed. "Escaping the death penalty," he said.

Reunited

We got to see mum, Lizzie and Sam again later that day. About an hour after Johnny left us, with a cheery "Don't worry, it'll all be fine" as he did, another agent unlocked our door and came in.

"Come on boys," he said, beckoning us outside. We didn't need further encouragement.

He took us down a long corridor, through some double doors and past an open courtyard. Here we realised it was actually dark – there'd been no windows to see out of since we had arrived – but there was no guessing what time it was, because, being February in Britain of course, it went dark early, even in another universe.

We went through another door, which was locked, and along a short corridor until we got to a large open room scattered with small tables and comfy armchairs. There was a red carpet on the floor, bookshelves and cupboards around the sides and an enormous TV in one corner, which was showing some programme about bees.

Sitting in the comfy chairs were mum, Lizzie and Sam. There were two other people, uniformed women, sat in a nearby corner, but otherwise the room was empty.

The man left us, saying nothing, but I wouldn't have heard him anyway, because by now mum had leapt to her feet and come to give me another huge hug.

"Thank God!" she started again, but I stopped her, saying: "I thought you didn't believe in God?"

She smiled at me, looking closely at my now clean face, and cupping my cheeks in her hands like I was a baby.

"Oh, I don't," she said, laughing now, "it's just a saying. Anyway, I've got to thank someone, haven't I?"

"Thank Johnny, then," I said, and she smiled again.

We all sat down again, and Lizzie shyly asked if she could sit on my knee. Although she was much too big for that now, I let her anyway. She weighed a ton, but I didn't mind. Jake sat glumly next to me.

We talked for a little about what had happened in the barn. Sam wanted to know why we thought DARTing would take us to safety, rather than sticking with the family – Jake, who had taken that decision, explained he just wanted to get away from the situation, and hadn't thought it may take us into even more danger.

We explained, rather excitedly, about where we had gone, about the different creatures there, and about losing the DART ("We wanted to come back, honestly!" said Jake), and Lizzie and mum kept gasping loudly at the peril we'd been in.

When we talked about Tin-o, and how he had saved us from starvation, Sam laughed and even mum raised a smile, while Lizzie wanted to know why we hadn't brought him back with us. "I'd love to have a dinosaur as a pet!" she shrieked down my ear. We told her that would not have been a good idea, even if we had been able to bring him home.

Sam said they already knew about the ‘evolved’ dinosaurs which had captured us, because Johnny had told them his side of the story. I wanted to know how the agent had found us – he hadn’t told us, and we had forgotten to ask earlier.

Sam explained: “Oh, he’d been tracking you for days. He found your – I mean, my – DART, soon after he got there, because as you know one DART can locate another. So he knew you had no way of returning, and, rather bravely I have to say, decided to try and find you.

“He followed your tracks for some way, but you seemed to be going all over the place and it wasn’t easy, despite his training. Apparently he thought he’d lost you at one point, then found your discarded tins and knew you must be somewhere near.”

“Good old Tin-o!” cheered Jake. I think he missed him.

“Anyway,” continued Sam, “it was just luck he

came across the trap you'd fallen into. You weren't there, but he found your rucksacks, and was able to follow the tracks the evolved dinosaurs made to their village."

"And he waited until night-time before rescuing us," guessed Jake.

Sam nodded. "It would've been too dangerous for all of you to attempt a rescue when the dinosaurs were around. He waited until they put you in the hut, with only one of them on guard."

"He didn't hurt the guard, did he?" asked Lizzie.

Sam shook his head. "He just knocked him out," said Sam, and Lizzie looked pleased.

"Hey, those things were going to eat us!" said Jake.

I frowned at him. "You don't know that! They just had no idea what we were, that's all," I said, looking over at Sam for help.

Sam shrugged his shoulders. "Who knows what they would've done?" he said. "They sound pretty primitive; I doubt, by the way they'd treated you so

far, that it would've ended well."

I shuddered. I dreaded to think what would've happened to us had Johnny not come along at the right time. At best we would have starved to death.

Mum started to change the subject, but Jake wanted to ask one more thing. "How come we came back here, to that room, when we DARTed with Johnny? And how come you were all waiting for us?"

I hadn't even thought of that, but when I did it confused me, too. I thought you DARTed to the same position – yet in another universe – that you left. We'd been somewhere near Oxford, hadn't we? Give or take the miles we had wandered from the original position.

Sam explained: "They've developed the technology quite a bit in the year or so I've been gone," he said. "There are now special DARTs which can be programmed to take you to specific places, not just universes. Johnny knew, when he DARTed with you, that he would be coming back here, to I-ART HQ, to that room – it's used for returning agents. We knew

you were coming back because they can also track the DARTs more easily now, even across universes. The agents here knew Johnny was returning with two people in tow."

"We knew you were coming!" shouted Lizzie, and I beamed at her. "We were soooo excited! But we had to wait two days! It was agony!"

"Two days?" I asked.

"Didn't you know? No, of course not…" said Sam. "The universe you were in is so far removed from ours that it took you just over two days to get there… and two days to get back, of course."

"Two days?" I repeated, in a slightly louder voice.

"Yup," said Sam.

I looked over at Jake, who seemed stunned. He opened his mouth, then shut it again, like a goldfish.

"So just how long have we been gone?" I asked, looking at mum this time.

"Ten days," she said, and there were tears in her eyes. "Ten horrible, agonising days."

....

We stayed together that evening (Sam informed us it was around eight o'clock) but were not allowed to talk about the trial.

When I tried to raise the subject Sam warned me with a glance, and one of the women sitting in the corner barked a "not allowed" at us. Apparently they were listening to every word, and, as Sam explained, if they thought we were talking about the trial they would make us separate again. We didn't want that.

So we chatted about the dinosaurs – Jake was very pleased to tell them what he had christened 'his' world – and Lizzie told us how boring it had been waiting for us to come back.

"They keep us locked up most of the time," she said, "and we only get to go out with someone following us. It's *very* boring here. There's no-one else to play with. It's alright for you, you were off having adventures!" I grinned at her.

After a while the I-ART staff allowed us to get

some games out of a cupboard, and we played a version of Monopoly until Jake and I started to yawn. Mum was fussing about how we must be shattered, about how we'd barely had any sleep in days – which was of course true, but adrenalin had kept us going – and asked the women if we could all have a nighttime drink.

I asked for hot chocolate, so naturally everyone else did, too, and one of the women went out and came back ten minutes later with a tray carrying five chocolatey drinks. Lizzie complained there were no marshmallows or chocolate sprinkles, but Jake and I fell about ours as if they were the best drinks we had ever tasted, which in a way they were.

After we'd drunk them, the I-ART women took us to our bedrooms: Sam, mum and Lizzie shared one room, while Jake and I were next door. The rooms were nice enough; not as well-furnished as a hotel, but clean and comfy, and there was a bathroom attached to each.

But when we'd said goodnight, undressed, put the

light out and got into bed, there was a click at the door, and I realised we had been locked in again.

Oh it was comfy, alright – and far, far better than sleeping up a tree – but it still felt like prison.

Questions

The next morning Jake and I slept late. I don't know what time it was when we woke, but the light streaming through the window – yes, this time we actually had a window – was bright and sunny.

I felt pretty refreshed, though a bit headachy, like you sometimes do when you've had too much sleep.

I looked over to where Jake was lying. He was staring at the ceiling, and grunted when I said "morning." Jake had never been a morning person, even if it was actually afternoon.

I got up, went to the bathroom and had a quick wash, before getting dressed. There was a small chest of drawers in-between the twin beds, and I opened them in turn. They were full of clothes, which, on closer inspection, were mine and Jake's.

"I think these are the clothes we had with us in the barn," I said. Jake was still in bed, and again grunted. I looked at him. "You OK, mate?" I asked.

He turned his head away, and I knew he was upset. I sat on his bed.

"You'll soon be home again," I said, although thinking it could really be a long time before we got back to our own universe.

Jake turned back to me. "Oh really?" he said. "We've already been gone more than two weeks. We've missed at least a week of school. We don't even know what day it is! My mum and dad will be frantic! They have no idea where I am – do you know how that feels?"

I shook my head, but tried to console him. "Hey," I said, "there's nothing we can do about it. You know they won't let us go before the trial. They don't care about your family. What are you going to do – escape?"

Jake looked serious, and I started panicking. "Oh no, Jake, there's no way you're going to be able to do that. What are you going to do, steal a DART?" I knew from experience that when my friend got an idea in his head he was reluctant to let it go. Remember Operation Lizzie? And look where that had got us – nearly killed by Sam's alternative reality brother Duncan.

Jake just grunted again, got out of bed and went into the bathroom.

I'd have to keep an eye on him to make sure he didn't do something stupid.

Soon after Jake had got dressed there was a click at the door, a token knock, and a woman in uniform came in.

"Oh good, you're awake," she said, stating the obvious. Why do grown-ups *do* that? They're always saying things like "my, you're tall," "it's really raining out there" and "you'll be sick if you eat any more chocolate."

The woman took us to the dining room we had previously used, gave us some breakfast (cereal, in case you're wondering), and told us we were going to be interviewed by the defence lawyer after we'd eaten.

This scared me a little, although I suppose I

shouldn't have been frightened. I mean, it's not like we were testifying for the prosecution, where what we said could put Sam in front of a firing squad.

Still, when the woman returned a little later and escorted us to another room I was really nervous. Come to think of it, giving evidence either way would presumably have an influence on the verdict. I didn't want anything I said to lead to Sam being found guilty.

We were put in a bare room with two wooden chairs, a small table and little else, and the I-ART woman went through another door, returning with a well-dressed lady who was obviously not an agent.

"This is Mrs Kennedy," said the woman. "She's Sam's defence lawyer. She'll be interviewing you both, but separately. It shouldn't take long." She then left, locking the door behind her.

Mrs Kennedy was a slim, attractive woman, probably in her 30s, though I'm not a good judge of age. She was dressed in a grey business suit and cream blouse, wore high heels and had neat short-ish brown hair. She looked just how I'd expect a lawyer to look. In a way this was reassuring.

She smiled at us both, told Jake to sit down and asked me to follow her to the adjoining room.

In the other room there were two more hard chairs and a table, nothing else. Mrs Kennedy sat down on one side of the table and gestured for me to sit on the other. I felt like you do when you get called in to see the headteacher at school – scared, and guilty even when you haven't done anything.

The lawyer had a folder on the desk in front of her, which she opened, and a small tape recorder, which she placed in front of me.

"Now then," she said, "do you know why you're here?" Her voice was kind and soft, but I was still frightened.

"Er," I stammered, but she didn't wait for me to go on.

"You're here because your friend Sam is about to go on trial," she continued, "for deserting his post the day he was due to be laid off, and for stealing two

DARTS, which were the property of I-ART."

I nodded, and she went on. "Now, the ultimate penalty for an agent deserting is death." I must have looked horrified – as indeed I was – for she hurriedly went on: "But we don't think it will come to that, thankfully." I sighed with relief.

"Since Sam left, I-ART has changed a lot. There's a new boss in charge, and there are new rules, some developments in technology and a fresh outlook on its aims and practices." I looked at her blankly, not knowing what she meant or what to say.

She seemed to sense this, for she went on: "Sam was not the only agent to desert that day. Quite a few of them went missing; most of them have not been found yet, and there is growing pressure to stop wasting time and money going looking for them; still, that's nothing to do with me, I'm glad to say."

She picked up a pen, plucked a form out of the folder on the table and looked at me. "I think there's a very good chance Sam will get off with a short spell in jail at worst, but if we can get him off completely that will obviously be a better outcome." She wrote something down on the form.

"So what I need from you is the details of how you met Sam, what he told you, how he acted and particularly if, in any way, he was helpful to you and your family."

I breathed a sigh of relief. Well, Sam had certainly been helpful to us – he'd not only given mum the medicine she needed to lead a normal life, but he'd actually saved mine and Jake's lives when we'd been in danger. I started to tell Mrs Kennedy this, but she quickly stopped me.

"From the beginning, please. Tell me everything – I can decide what's important later. I'm going to tape everything you say, so I can listen to it again. Just try to keep to the facts." And she pressed the tape recording button. "When did you first meet Sam?"

I settled back in my chair, took a deep breath, and told her everything.

It took me a while, but I wasn't tired when I had finished my tale.

Mrs Kennedy sat, listening and taking occasional notes, nodding at some of the best bits. She sometimes asked me a question, when I hadn't been explaining properly, but mainly she just let me talk. It felt good to tell someone.

When I got to the end – she wanted to know what had happened since we left home to run away from the agents, too, although she asked me to skip over the Dinoworld adventure, seeing as it didn't involve Sam – she turned the tape recorder off, and stood up.

"OK, thank you Ethan," she said. "I'll probably want to speak to you again, before the trial, so I can tell you what I'll be asking you about on the witness stand."

I stood up too, my knees protesting because I'd been sitting down so long. "You mean I have to get up in court?" I asked. The thought terrified me.

"Oh yes," said the lawyer. "You're a character

witness. Both I and the prosecution lawyer will be asking you questions, but don't worry; you just have to tell the truth, that's all."

That didn't make me feel any better, but she showed me out to the room where Jake had been waiting. He had had nothing to do, and looked glad to see us.

As he passed me on the way into his interview, I whispered: "Good luck!" He looked scared, too.

The door shut behind him, and I was alone for what seemed like an eternity. Why was there never anything to look at in these rooms? Did the people in this universe not need distractions?

I was counting the tiles on the floor for the second time (54) when there was a click in the lock and the main door opened. The same woman as before came in, followed by a girl of about 14 or 15.

"Sit down," the woman ordered, and the girl sat in the chair next to me. The woman then left, locking the door as usual.

The girl immediately turned to me. She had long,

straight blonde hair with lots of thin blue streaks, big blue eyes ringed by black eyeliner, and lips covered in purple lipstick. Tall and skinny, she was wearing a grey hoodie, black jeans and black and white baseball boots.

"Oo are you then?" she asked. Her accent was a bit strange, although I felt I'd heard it before.

"Er," I stammered.

The girl got up without waiting for me to answer, went to the window and immediately tried to open it. It was locked, and she swore softly.

"What are you doing?" I asked.

She looked at me as if I was stupid. "Tryin' to escape, of course," she said. "What, d'you think I'm goin' to stay here if I can help it? I've got much more important things to be doing." She gave up trying to open the window and looked around. The room was bare.

"Great," she said, and sat down again. She started to pick at her sleeve.

"So who *are* you?" she asked again.

"Ethan Jones," I said.

"You got somethin' to do with Sam?" she asked.

I started. "Yes. I'm his friend. Do you know Sam too?"

The girl blinked at me. Her eyelashes were obviously false. "Yeah, I know Sam. He's my uncle."

I stared at her, not understanding.

"My uncle?" she went on, "you know, my dad's brother?"

I must have looked idiotic, because she continued: "I'm Duncan's daughter."

Mia

Duncan's *daughter*? *The* Duncan? The alternative version of Sam from another universe, a fellow agent who had some sort of grudge against him and had tried to steal his DART? I didn't know he had a daughter (though why would I?)

I sat there, open-mouthed, and the girl laughed loudly.

"So you know who my dad is, then, judgin' by the look on your face," she said. That's where I had heard that accent before.

"I… er… we have met, yes," I said. I remembered him sitting on my back, pressing my face to the dusty floor of the coastguard house, and frowned.

The girl just shrugged, obviously not interested in the details. "He gets around," was all she said, before digging her hand into her hoodie pocket and pulling out a packet of chewing gum. I didn't recognise the brand. She took one out, unwrapped it and put it in her mouth, before offering me one. I said no thanks, and she put the packet away.

"What's your name again?" she asked me.

"Ethan. Ethan Jones," I said.

She screwed up her face, as if she was trying to remember something, then shook her head. "No, never 'eard of you," she said.

I was quite annoyed, for some reason. The last time I had seen her father, he had been pointing a gun at me.

"What's *your* name?" I asked, a little tetchily.

"Mia," came the short reply.

"OK, Mia," I said, suddenly needing answers. "What are you doing here in this universe if you're from Duncan's world?"

"Same as you, I s'pect," she said, through her gum. "I'm supposed to be givin' evidence for Sam."

I stared, and she went on, in a bored tone: "Sam did my mum and me a favour, oh, a few years ago now, and he's calling me as a character witness. The agents came and got me just as I was having the best fun of my life, so I'm not very 'appy about it. But still, anythin' to help Sam, I suppose…" she trailed off, and my head was reeling with questions. What favour did Sam do for her? How was this related to Duncan's hatred of him?

I was about to ask her, when the door opened again and Mrs Kennedy and Jake came back in. Jake looked drained, and not very happy. He seemed shocked to see someone else in the room with me.

"Oh, hello again, Mia," said Mrs Kennedy. "Could you go into that room, please, and stay there while I just go and get someone to take the boys back. I won't be long." Mia did as she was told, but pulled tongues at the lawyer's back. I was too shocked to laugh.

Mrs Kennedy took a key out of her jacket pocket, unlocked the other door and went out, locking it behind her.

Immediately Mia came back in from the other room. "Oo are you then?" she asked Jake. My friend looked at me, confused, and I pointed at the girl. "This is Mia, Jake. Apparently she's Duncan's daughter, and no, she's not very polite."

Mia laughed, swore at me, then went to stand by the window, looking out. "God, I hate it here!" she yelled suddenly, making Jake and I jump. "It's boring as… even worse than our HQ, and that's saying something. Jeez! I wish they'd hurry up and get the trial over with. I'm not waiting around much longer, I tell you, Sam or not."

Jake was looking at me expectantly, so I explained Mia was a character witness for Sam, too.

"What did the lawyer ask you, then?" I asked Jake.

He tore his eyes away from our fellow prisoner, who he had been staring at in some bemusement, and sort of shook his head. "She'd already got most of the story from you, I think," he said, "so she just wanted me to fill in my details. I told her how Sam helped save us, of course, and how he never wanted us to use the DART; that it was our fault we got into trouble."

There was a snort from Mia, and we turned to her. "What?" I asked.

She was looking at us like we were little boys,

which of course irritated me (although to her, I suppose, we were little boys).

"Adults never want you to use the DARTs, do they? It's like they want to have all the fun themselves," she said.

"Oh, I suppose you've used them lots, have you?" asked Jake unbelievingly.

"I stole my first one when I was just eight," she said, and I rolled my eyes. Jake laughed. "Oh yeah?"

"Yeah," she said.

"And I bet you've been everywhere, have you?"

"I've been to lots of places, yeah," she said. "I've seen things you wouldn't believe!"

I groaned. This was beginning to sound like an argument.

"Oh yeah?" retorted Jake. "Like what?"

"Like Nazis marching through London, like flying cars and household robots, like ape people, like…" she paused, thinking. "*Ape* people?" I murmured.

"We went to a land full of dinosaurs!" shouted Jake, hoping to out-do her.

Mia laughed – this time a genuine, full-on laugh, which made her face light up. She actually started crying with laughter, wiping her eyes, mascara streaking down her face.

"No way!" she said when she had got herself under control again.

Jake was laughing too. "Way!" he said, and I started laughing as well.

"How the hell did you end up there?" she asked, still giggling. "One of the first things you learn is not to go to the Six Zeroes. Jeez! That is precious!"

"We sort of went there by accident," said Jake, "and then we lost the DART, so we got stuck."

This made Mia laugh even more, and she was still laughing two minutes later when Mrs Kennedy returned, bringing a young male agent with her.

"I thought I told you to wait in that room," said the lawyer sternly, pointing at the door.

"Well, I thought I told you I have a problem with authority," said Mia through her laughter, and I couldn't help smiling.

Mrs Kennedy ushered her into the room, followed her, shut the door, and we went out with the man. Jake and I were still laughing when he showed us back to our bedroom.

We talked about Mia a lot that day, but we didn't see her again until the trial.

....

It wasn't until the evening that we were allowed to see mum, Lizzie and Sam again, in the same 'visiting room' as before. One of the first things we talked about was Mia. I wanted to ask Sam all about her, but he just smiled.

"I'll let Mia tell her own story," he said. "Suffice to say I tried to help her and her mum out once, and although it didn't go to plan, you could say I saved her life."

He did want to know how she was, though. "I haven't seen her for years," he said, sadly. "It's nice to know she's doing OK. She sounds as stroppy as when

I first met her."

"But how come Duncan hates you if you saved his daughter's life?" asked Jake. It was a good question, and one I was about to ask myself.

Sam sighed. "Duncan's got a lot to be upset about," he said. "He blames me for… well, for his wife's death, although it wasn't my fault." Lizzie and mum gasped, and mum put her hand on Sam's arm.

"Do you want to tell us about it, Sam?" asked mum gently.

Sam shook his head. "It's a long story, and I'd rather not dwell on it here. Now who's up for another game of Monopoly?"

So we played a game, Lizzie cheating as usual, and avoided talking about the trial, until it was time for bed.

That night I dreamt of Mia.

In court

It was another three days until the trial. Another three days of sitting around, trying to keep ourselves entertained (after much complaining on our part, the agents eventually gave us TVs in our rooms, as well as some books and a few games, so we could at least have something to do.)

We only got to meet up with mum, Sam and Lizzie for a couple of hours each evening – they didn't trust us not to talk, apparently, so we didn't eat together. It really felt like being in prison.

The only other person we saw was Mrs Kennedy. At our second meeting she told us what would happen in the trial; that we would be called individually, and she would ask us some questions about Sam. The prosecution may ask us questions, too, but she couldn't be sure. She gave us an idea of what type of things she would be asking, but couldn't tell us details because that wasn't allowed.

The evening before the trial Sam was exceptionally nervous. He barely spoke for most of the time we were together, and he kept staring into space. Mum was obviously unsettled, too, but she kept making encouraging remarks to keep our spirits up. They didn't work. How could they? We all knew that the following day Sam may, at the very least, be taken away from us forever, and sent to jail. At the worst… well, we all hoped it wouldn't come to that, but it was still in our minds.

That night was a bad one. I don't think any of us slept much.

When we woke up on the day of the trial, our regular lady agent told us to dress in our smartest clothes, to make a good impression, and then took us to breakfast as usual. But instead of leading us back to our room once we'd eaten, she escorted us out of the building and into a car.

We hadn't been outside the HQ since we got there, and it was nice to be out, even if we were scared of where we were going.

The car was a make I didn't recognise. It was black, large and roomy, and a male agent sat in the back, in-between Jake and I.

"Where are we going?" asked Jake, as soon as we set off. Outside, the sun was shining, although it was quite cold and they hadn't allowed us to get our coats.

"Court," said the agent. He wasn't one for talking, then.

"Will it take long?" my friend asked.

"About an hour," came the reply.

"And when we get there, will we go in straight away?" Jake was full of questions this morning. I just wanted to get it over with as soon as possible; my stomach was churning with worry.

This time the agent turned to look at him, his face serious. "Just be quiet, please," he said. Well, that was the end of that conversation.

As we drove along I looked out of the window at this familiar, but really alien, universe. Although it wasn't strange that I didn't recognise anywhere, it was odd to think that this world was actually not our own; that there were things in it that I wouldn't understand, and that somewhere not far away there was another version of my mum, dad and Lizzie, as well as an alternative version of me, living a life I knew little about.

I briefly wondered what would happen if mum and Lizzie – my versions of them – met the ones Jake and I had seen last summer, when we journeyed to Sam's universe. Although I knew from experience they looked very similar, they were in fact different, as Sam had explained it was not possible to DART into a reality where the exact same version of you existed. Still, it would have made for an interesting meeting.

I scanned the streets and roads for signs that this was a different world from my own, but saw nothing, apart from posters for films and brands I had never heard of, and that was not jarringly unusual; it was a bit like being in a foreign country.

We arrived at the court soon enough. It was on the edge of a town centre; a large red brick building with huge double entrance doors and a polished brass sign to one side which said Huntington Marshall Court.

The agent led us out of the car and up the steps to the entrance, then inside to a large open foyer. There were two staircases opposite the door, and people milling around looking important.

The agent walked us over to a reception desk, had a word with the man behind it, then took us up the stairs to the first floor.

"We're in court number 4," he said, accompanying us along a dark corridor before stopping at a closed door with '4' on it. He knocked. A woman opened the door, spoke quietly to the agent, looked at us, nodded her head and then showed us in.

Inside was a large, open room with a high ceiling and huge windows allowing the sunlight to flood in. It was a typical courtroom like you see on TV, with a raised platform to the front and rows of chairs and tables facing it. There were people already here, sitting in various places, and I saw Mrs Kennedy close to the front, sat at a table with another woman. She had a folder and a glass of water in front of her, and as we came in she smiled at us.

The agent showed us to a bench at the side of the room, and we sat down. As we did the door opened and several other people came in. Some of them were accompanied by I-ART staff, who you could tell by their dark uniforms, while others seemed to be on their own. They all sat down, and soon the room was half-full of people, many talking quietly.

A large black man wearing a smart suit sat in front of me, and as he did he looked around at Jake and I and smiled. I didn't know who he was, but I smiled back anyway. Jake mouthed a "who is he?" at me, and I shrugged my shoulders.

After about five minutes the door opened again, and I saw Mia being brought in by two women agents. She was wearing the same hoodie and jeans as before, but her hair was tied up in an untidy bun on top of her head. Blue streaks stuck out at odd angles.

She obviously needed more of a guard than we did – perhaps they didn't trust her not to run away – for they held her elbows as she came in and manoeuvred her to a bench two rows down from where we were sitting.

She didn't look in our direction, so we didn't have a chance to wave.

I was just looking round for mum and Lizzie – surely they would be in here too? – when one of the official-looking people at the front of the room shouted: "Be upstanding for Judge Harrison Jackson," and we all stood up.

The judge was a thin, small, middle-aged white man with a bald head, wearing a black robe lined with dark purple and carrying a brown briefcase. He entered the room through a door above the raised platform, and sat down on a large black chair which made him look even smaller. He waved his free hand dismissively in our direction as he sat down, and we all obediently sat.

He opened his briefcase on the desk in front of him, plucked out some papers, read a few of them, then beckoned Mrs Kennedy and the other woman up to his seat. They had to walk up two steps to get there.

After a brief talk to them, he sat upright and cleared his throat. Everyone immediately went quiet.

"We are here to hear the case of I-ART against former agent Samuel Harding, the first charge being one of absconding from duty, albeit on the day he was to be dismissed, and the more serious charge of stealing two DARTs, being the property of I-ART. Anyone who's in the wrong courtroom, please leave now." He paused. No-one moved.

"Good," he went on. "Please bring in the prisoner."

My heart skipped a beat. One of the officials, who were dressed in black uniforms not unlike the agents, but with different logos on their jackets and thin yellow piping down their trouser legs, went out of yet another door and returned with Sam, flanked by two agents.

They took him over to a slightly raised platform to one side of the judge. He stood there, looking strained and worried, and my heart went out to him. He was wearing his best suit, I noticed – one he had bought for job interviews. I wondered where he'd got it from – surely he hadn't taken it with him when we started running? I tried to smile at him, but he was looking the other way.

The judge turned to him. "Could you please state your name for the court?"

Sam cleared his throat, looked up at the ceiling, and said in a surprisingly strong voice: "Samuel Harding."

"Samuel Harding, you stand accused of two counts under the laws of this country: That one, you knowingly and deliberately absconded from your duty as an agent for the Institute for Alternative Reality Technology, henceforth referred to as I-ART; and secondly, that you knowingly and deliberately stole two Devices for Alternative Reality Transportation, henceforth referred to as DARTs. Do you understand the charges?"

Sam said he did.

"How do you plead?"

I held my breath.

“Guilty, Your Honour,” said Sam.

I gasped, as did Jake at my side. Guilty? What? I didn't understand.

The judge made a shushing noise as the people in the courtroom started to murmur among themselves. Presumably not many people had expected that. We all fell silent, and I stared at Sam. He still wasn't looking in my direction, but he looked calm enough.

The judge spoke up: "Samuel Harding, you have pleaded guilty to the charges put to you, so we will now hear from your character witnesses before we make a judgement as to your punishment. Call the first witness."

One of the officials read from a piece of paper in her hand, calling out: "Call Damien Wilmslow."

At this, the black man in front of us, who had smiled at Jake and I when he sat down, rose and made his way to the front, where he was directed to a stand close to our friend. He nodded at Sam as he took his place, I noticed.

"Can you please state your name for the court," said the judge.

"Damien Wilmslow," said the man. He had a London accent, and his voice was deep and calm.

"And what is your occupation?" asked the judge.

"Security consultant," said Damien.

The judge went on: "I will now hand you over to the defence for questioning. Mrs Kennedy?"

Our old friend Mrs Kennedy stood up and went to stand in front of Damien. She had a notebook in her hand, which she kept looking at. I presumed she had notes on there.

"How do you know Samuel Harding, Mr Wilmslow?" she asked.

Damien glanced over at Sam, before saying: "He and I were in the Army together, ma'am, for five years." Mrs Kennedy smiled, said: "You don't need to call me that," then went on: "Can you tell us what kind of a person Samuel is?"

Damien smiled. "He's a kind, honest, genuine and

principled man, ma'am. He's the best friend a man could ever have, ma'am… I mean, Mrs…"

Mrs Kennedy interrupted him. "And can you tell the court what happened on the day of…" she looked down at her notes, "August 22nd, 1988?"

The man sort of settled himself down, looked at his feet, then told us his tale: "On that day Sam and I were both in Egypt, serving in the British Army. We had known each other for a couple of years, and were in the same regiment. We were friends as well as comrades.

"We'd been sent to Egypt five months before as part of the British defence of the country against the dictator Arol Naback. Our mission was to help the Egyptian people repel Naback's advances."

He paused to take breath, then went on: "On the morning of August 22nd we were involved in a skirmish with some of Naback's troops, and only narrowly escaped. In the chaos of retreating I got separated from the rest of our unit, and ended up alone and disorientated.

"The sun was fierce, I had been injured – I had a slight arm injury – and I started to wander – in the wrong direction, as it turned out. I had lost my gun in the battle, and would be defenceless if found by the enemy."

He paused again, and Mrs Kennedy said: "If you need to take a drink, there's water there for you."

"I'm fine, thank you" said Damien, and he went on: "I must have wandered for about half a mile, when there was a shout from behind me, and I realised I'd walked into an ambush. Immediately I was surrounded by Naback's men. There were six or seven of them, all heavily armed.

"I raised my arms in surrender, and when they realised I had no weapons they grabbed me and marched me at gunpoint to their camp two miles away, which was in a place the locals called Devil's Bridge."

Devil's Bridge! I suddenly knew who Damien was – why I hadn't remembered the name earlier I don't know; there was so much going on in my head it had gone clean out. Of course; Damien was Sam's friend from his own reality who he said owed him a favour, and who he had told us to contact if we ever needed help, using the code 'Devil's Bridge' to indicate we were friends.

I looked round at Jake, but he was too intent on the story being told to notice me.

Damien was continuing with his tale. "I suppose they wanted to keep me as a hostage," he said, "because at that time a lot of hostages were being taken and demands being made for their release. Most of the hostages ended up dead.

"So they tied my wrists and feet together and put me in a tent in their camp." I shivered, remembering how that had felt when Jake and I had been captured by the dinosaurians, although it seemed like years ago now.

Damien went on: "Night came, and it looked like I was going to be there a while. They gave me a little food and water, untying my hands for a time to let me eat and drink, but otherwise ignored me."

Mrs Kennedy butted in: “There was little hope of rescue, was there not?”

Damien barked a short laugh. “Well, I was in the enemy camp, there were about 50 of Naback’s heavily armed men around me; no commander would ever attempt a rescue mission, even had they known where I was. It was understood that if you got captured, you were on your own. I truly thought I’d never see home again.”

Mrs Kennedy nodded, then said: “And can you tell us what happened that night?”

The man shook his head. “I still don’t know how he did it, ma’am, I mean, Miss… but Sam rescued me. It had gone dark, I was dozing off in my tent, still tied up, when I heard a noise outside. There was a thud, and someone entered the tent, dragging something heavy. I couldn’t see much – the desert is pretty dark at night, you know, and there weren’t many lights on in the camp.

“Suddenly the man who had come in whispered in

my ear that I was to be quiet if I valued my life. I recognised the voice as Sam's, but would have obeyed it anyway. I mean, I know when to take orders." Damien smiled again, then continued: "Sam had a knife, which he used to cut the rope at my wrists. He then handed me the knife and I cut the one tying my ankles while he kept watch at the door of the tent.

"When I was free I stood up and promptly tripped over a body on the floor. Sam had killed the man guarding the tent and dragged his body inside so it wouldn't be seen." Intent though I was on the story, I still had time to shudder when I heard that Sam had killed a man. Still, he had been at war, I expect he had killed several people. The thought horrified me.

Damien was continuing: "Sam led me out of the camp, back the way he had come, without incident. We didn't meet anyone else. Most of them were asleep or drunk by then. Anyway, as soon as we were clear of the camp I asked Sam how he'd found me, and he just shrugged and said as soon as he knew I was missing he had come looking for me, eventually found some tracks and followed them back to the camp.

"I asked him why he'd come alone, and he said he had the best chance of rescuing me alone. I knew then he hadn't asked for permission to rescue me – and sure enough, when we got back to base we had to make up some story about him finding me while out on patrol. If they had known Sam had come to get me he would have been in big trouble."

Damien had finished his story, and stopped. "Do you want me to add anything else, Miss?" he asked.

Mrs Kennedy shook her head. "No, thank you, Mr Wilmslow, that will be all. Do you have any questions, Miss Thornton?" and she turned to the lady who had been sitting beside her.

Miss Thornton, who was younger, shorter and rather plump, got up from her desk and went to stand in front of Damien. Mrs Kennedy sat down.

"Mr Wilmslow," she said, "would you say that Samuel Harding did a reckless thing in rescuing you?"

Damien blinked twice, then said: "Well, there is a risk in any military mission, ma'am, but Sam knew what he was doing. He saved my life."

Miss Thornton coughed gently. "But you cannot deny that he rescued you against orders from his superior officers; they would not have allowed him to risk his life in order to rescue you, would they?"

Sam's friend blinked again. "I can't deny he was acting against orders, no..."

"Thank you, Mr Wilmslow, that will be all."

Damien was about to say something else, but he was ushered out of the stand and back to his seat close to Jake and I.

The judge wrote something down on a piece of paper in front of him, then looked at his notes again.

"Call the next witness," he said.

The same official as before read her notes, then said: "Call Mia McGregor."

My heart leaped. It was Mia's turn.

Mia's tale: 1

Mia got up slowly and walked over to the stand, accompanied by one of the agents. She stood where Damien had been a moment before. She was chewing gum, and she looked bored.

The judge turned to her and said: "Can you please state your name for the court."

Mia chewed a little more, then drawled: "Mia McGregor."

"Are you chewing gum, Miss McGregor?" asked the judge. He sounded like my teachers.

Mia stared at him. "Yep," she said. "Why, d'you want some?"

Someone in the audience laughed, but the judge was not amused. "Take it out, please," he said sternly. An official walked up to Mia, put her hand out in front of Mia's face, and the teenager spat her gum out into the hand. I smiled a little. She really didn't like authority, did she?

The judge asked her how old she was – “14,” she said – then went on: “I will now hand you over to the defence for questioning.”

Mrs Kennedy went to stand in front of Mia, note-book in her hand again. “Can you please tell us what universe you originate from?” Now that was a question you didn’t hear in our world, I thought.

Straight away, Mia said: “367,930,552,169.” She said the numbers like they were a telephone number, without the ‘million’ or ‘thousands.’

“And can you tell us how you know the number of your own reality so well?” asked the lawyer.

Mia sort of blinked, her long false eyelashes fluttering like butterflies. She sneered a little. “Well, I ’ad to learn it, didn’t I?” she said.

Mrs Kennedy shifted her weight from one foot to the other. “Why did you have to learn it?” she said.

“Because I want to be able to go ’ome if I’m in trouble,” said Mia.

Mrs Kennedy turned to the judge – I suddenly realised there was no obvious jury; maybe there wasn’t one. Maybe the judge was deciding the punishment.

"I want to explain a little about the background to Mia's evidence, if I may, Your Honour," she said.

"Of course," said the judge, "I don't want to be here all day, and I suspect getting information out of your witness will be like extracting blood out of the proverbial stone." I had a feeling he was right. Mia didn't seem the co-operative type.

Mrs Kennedy started: "Mia's father, Duncan McGregor, is the AR brother (the alternative reality brother, that is) of Samuel Harding. Samuel and he met by accident while Samuel was on a mission to Duncan's reality. Apparently Samuel had tracked down his parents, who were dead in his own reality, in order that he could see them again."

At this, the judge butted in: "That is highly irregular, is it not?" he said.

"It is against I-ART policy, yes," said Mrs Kennedy, "but Samuel checked that he had never existed in their reality before he met them, so he didn't cause them distress. He pretended to be someone else, just so he could get to see them again. It was a sentimental thing, Your Honour; he never meant any harm to come from it."

The judge grunted, and I got the impression he wasn't impressed by Sam's behaviour.

"As Samuel was leaving his parents' house, he unfortunately encountered Duncan, who is, of course, Samuel's AR parents' son, and an agent for the I-ART that exists in that reality.

"Duncan guessed something was unusual about his parents' visitor, and they had an argument."

I looked at Mia, but she was just staring into space, as if bored by the whole process. I suppose she already knew this story.

Mrs Kennedy went on: "Anyway, to cut a long story short," (I heard the judge mumble "please do") "Duncan ended up taking Samuel back to his home to question him further. Here, Samuel met Duncan's wife, Gail, and daughter, Mia, who were there unexpectedly. I will now return to questioning the witness."

She turned back to Mia. "Could you tell us how old you were when you first met Samuel Harding?" Mia: "Seven."

"And can you tell us what happened when Samuel Harding came to your house for the first time?"

Mia sighed. "Well, dad was all for turnin' him over to I-ART, wasn't he?"

"I don't know, Mia, that's why I'm asking you. Please just tell us what happened, as concisely as you can."

Mia sighed again. "Well, me and mum had got in early, so dad didn't expect us to be there. He brought Sam in and started to ask 'im questions about who 'e was and why 'e was visiting grandma and grandad. Things got nasty, and mum was tryin' to get dad to let Sam go, but he wouldn't – dad was goin' to get the agents to arrest him, and Sam just wanted to go 'ome."

"So what happened next?" asked Mrs Kennedy.

Mia continued: "Well, in the end mum let Sam escape while dad's back was turned, but 'e couldn't go back 'ome because dad had taken his DARTs."

"And your father was angry at this, yes?" asked the lawyer.

"God, he was fumin' of course," said Mia, and someone in the room giggled.

"Did your father often get angry with you and your mum?" asked Mrs Kennedy.

Mia laughed. It wasn't a happy laugh. "All the time," she said. "He used to rant at us whenever he was 'ome, although thankfully that wasn't very often, cos he worked as an agent."

"Yes, we know that," said Mrs Kennedy. "Can you tell us what happened a week later, please?"

"Well, dad had gone somewhere – I don't know where – and mum told me we were goin' away." She looked sad when she was telling this.

"She was taking you to another reality, wasn't she?" asked the lawyer.

"Well, I didn't know that at first, but yeah, she wanted me and her to go somewhere else, to get away from dad."

"Why did she want to get away?"

Mia looked blank. "Well I don't know, I was only seven," she said.

Mrs Kennedy looked down at her notebook, presumably for inspiration. "You told me that she had often talked about leaving home, about escaping the life you and she had, because it wasn't very pleasant, is that right?"

"Well yeah," said Mia. "Dad wouldn't let mum work; she was stuck in the house all day. She hated our universe, and dad kept tellin' her about all these other places that were far better, where everyone was happy, but 'e wouldn't take us there – said it was against the rules, and that we should be glad he was payin' for a roof over our 'eads."

She paused, and Mrs Kennedy asked: "Can you now tell us about the second time you saw Samuel Harding, please."

Mia looked down at her feet, and I thought she may have been trying not to cry, tough though she appeared. "Well, mum had already packed us some stuff, in a couple of bags, and she took me out to the park down the road. When we got there, Sam was waitin'. I didn't know it, but he and mum had been talkin' about leaving."

"Let me get this straight, Mia," said Mrs Kennedy. "Since you had last seen Samuel, he and your mother had been communicating, and they had hatched a plan together, is that right?"

Mia nodded. "Yeah. Mum was to give Sam his DARTs back – dad had hidden them in the house, but mum knew where they were – and Sam was to help us escape to another universe. He was goin' to take us somewhere nice, where we could live forever. Without dad."

I was shocked by this, thinking how Sam had told us not to interfere with other people's lives. Then again, he had certainly interfered with ours.

"So what happened next?"

Mia looked sad again. "Well, that's where it all went wrong, see? It wasn't Sam's fault," – she turned to the judge when she said this – "really, it wasn't his fault at all; nothing that happened was his fault… but it all went wrong."

"What happened that day, Mia?" asked Mrs Kennedy. Her voice was suddenly gentle, and a chill passed through me.

Mia looked at her. "That's when we lost mum," she said, quietly.

Mia's tale: 2

I started a little, remembering how Sam had told us Duncan blamed him for his wife's death.

Mrs Kennedy was asking Mia another question: "Can you please tell us, as concisely as you can, what happened that day – and stick with the facts, please."

Mia sort of crumpled up her mouth, as if sucking her teeth, coughed, then told us her tale.

"We sat down in the park with Sam. I remember it was really sunny, and there were two little piglets running around, playin'. He showed us how the DARTs work – how you open them, and how you programme them – and got us to memorise our reality's number, so's we could return if we needed to. We had to repeat it several times without making a mistake before he'd let us go anywhere.

"Then he gave mum one of his DARTs, told her she could keep it, and got her to programme in the place he was takin' us to. He said he couldn't do it, cos his DARTs would just take him 'ome."

"And how did you decide where to escape to?" asked the lawyer.

"Well, Sam had a notebook with details of every reality he'd ever been to – its reality number, what it was like, any differences he'd found, how long 'e had stayed there, you know, everythin' he needed to know.

"He'd looked through this notebook and picked a reality he thought we'd do OK in – they 'ad the same passport system and money as us, so we could take cash and our ID with us and not have to worry about gettin' new ones."

"That would make it easier for you to settle down in a new universe, right?" asked Mrs Kennedy.

Mia nodded. "Apparently mum had taken all our money out of the bank – that was what was in one of the bags – and had our passports and other stuff we'd need to make a new life.

"Sam said he'd been to this reality he was takin' us to some years ago, when he first started as an agent, but he thought it was safe, and everyone had been nice and friendly." She paused.

"He thought it was safe," she repeated, and she looked sad again.

Mrs Kennedy took a step towards her. "So your mum programmed the DART, and you all DARTed to this other world, yes? What happened then?"

"When we got there, Sam took us to a hotel, where we checked in and went to a room. It was a bit of a dump, but Sam said it'd be alright for a couple of days while 'e checked the place out. He was goin' to stay with us until we were settled.

"So mum and I stayed in the hotel room while Sam went out to get more information. He came back after an hour with two phones – one for mum, one for him – so we could communicate if we needed to."

"Because your own phones would not work in another reality, I suppose," said Mrs Kennedy. Mia nodded again. "Can you tell us what happened next?"

"Sam went out again, and mum and I watched TV.

There were some channels on there we didn't recognise, and we were laughin' at some programmes talkin' about stuff we didn't know existed. You know, it was excitin' to be in another reality. We'd never done it before.

"Sam was away a long time, and we got bored. A hotel room is boring after a while, even in another world. Mum went down to reception to ask if they could get us some food, and that… and that's when the men came." She stopped.

"What men, Mia? Who came?"

Mia breathed in hard. It was obviously painful for her to remember.

"There was a knock at the door, and two men barged in. I didn't let them in, they just came in. They shouted at me to go with them. I had no idea who they were – they said mum was ill, and I had to go with them.

"Well, I was only seven, and scared, so I did. One of them grabbed our bags, and took them with us. We got down the stairs, and they took me outside to a van, where they put me in the back. One of them got in with me. There were no seats, and it was dark. It smelled like paint."

She paused, and Mrs Kennedy told her to drink some water if she wanted. Mia shook her head, and went on.

"I kept askin' them where mum was, and they kept sayin' they were takin' me to her. But of course they weren't. We drove for about five minutes, then they stopped and got me out. They pushed me into another hotel. This one was even dirtier than the first, and it stank. I didn't want to go, but they made me."

"And your mother wasn't there, was she?" asked Mrs Kennedy.

Mia shook her head, a bit tearful now at the memory. I didn't blame her. It must have been terrifying.

"They had in fact kidnapped you, had they not? For reasons unascertained, the men had taken you from one hotel to another, leaving your mother to wonder where you were. What do you remember happening next?"

Mia sighed. "Well, they took me up some stairs, put me in a room, locked the door and told me to shut up," she said. "I made a lot of noise, but they ignored me. I was there for ages – I tried to escape, but the window was too high from the ground, and there was no other way out.

"Some time later the two men came back to give me some food, but I threw it on the floor. They were angry, and kept yelling at me. I don't remember what they said."

"You were there for several hours, from what I can gather," said Mrs Kennedy, "before Sam and your mother appeared suddenly at the door. Can you tell us what happened?"

Mia sighed again. "The men were in the room with me, arguin' about somethin' I didn't understand, when there was a knock at the door. One of them went to answer it, and when he opened the door he got pushed inside.

"I turned round to look and saw it was Sam. He had a knife. He grabbed one of the men and they started fightin'. Then mum came in, and she rushed over to me and hugged me. She was crying.

"Sam was shoutin' at us to get out, to run, but then more men arrived, and one of them had a gun. I can't remember what happened, really – there was lots of shouting, and fighting, and… and everyone was all over the place. I just wanted to go 'ome."

Mrs Kennedy was pacing up and down. She stopped, and turned to Mia again.

"I know it's painful for you, Mia, but you need to tell us what happened next."

Mia blinked again, eyelashes damp now. "Well, the man with the gun grabbed mum away from me, and pointed the gun at her head. I was screamin' and ran to the door, where Sam was on the floor with another man on top of him. They stopped fightin'.

"The man with the gun shouted somethin' about shooting mum, and Sam got up, dropped his knife, and stood next to me. He told them to let us all go, and said they could keep our money instead. They laughed at him. One of them said the money was a bonus.

"No-one seemed to know what to do next. The man with the gun, who I think was in charge, told another to go and get Gary. I dunno who Gary was.

"As he was goin' out, Sam suddenly grabbed my arm, put his hand in his pocket, and shouted to mum: 'Use the DART!' I saw mum pick her DART out of her pocket – she was wearing a flowery dress with pockets in the front – and she looked me in the eye. She looked scared. Then I saw her press the button, and she disappeared. The man pointing the gun at her swore."

Mia stopped again, obviously distressed. Mrs Kennedy, her voice gentle, urged her to go on.

"As soon as he saw mum had gone, Sam pushed his DART button, and the room went black… me and him DARTed back 'ome.

"And… and that was the last time I saw mum."

The trial ends

I was gripped by the story, eyes only on Mia's face, and I noticed she was definitely blinking back tears by now.

Then Mrs Kennedy stood in front of her, so my view of her was blocked. "You and Sam returned to your universe, but there was no sign of your mother. Is that correct?"

Mia said quietly: "Yeah. We expected her to be there. She should have been there – she had DARTed a second before we did – I saw her disappear. She should have been there, but she wasn't."

"So what did you do then?" the lawyer's voice was gentle and kind.

"Well, Sam took me 'ome. In case mum had gone there somehow, although she should've DARTed in the same place as us. But she wasn't there. And we couldn't get in anyway, cos we didn't 'ave a key.

"Sam left me with a neighbour, and went off to

look for mum. He DARTed back to the universe we'd come from, and looked around, but there was no sign."

"He put himself in more danger in order to look for your mother, did he not?" asked Mrs Kennedy.

Mia nodded. "He spent days lookin' for her, trying to find out where she could have gone to, but it was no use. There was no sign. No-one's seen her since."

I felt sick to the stomach. Imagine having someone you love just disappear, never to be seen again. It must be dreadful not knowing what happened to them.

Mrs Kennedy turned towards the judge. "Samuel Harding spent the next three days searching for Mrs McGregor, to no avail. He even went back to the hotel where the kidnappers had been, putting himself in great danger, but there was no sign of her. In the end he concluded her DART had malfunctioned, and she had somehow gone to another universe, without being able to return. It was impossible to trace her with the technology available at the time.

"After looking for Mrs McGregor for some time, he then returned to make sure Mia was alright. Again putting himself in danger – for, of course, Mia had by this time been reunited with her father, Duncan, who was not at all pleased to learn of the events that had taken place while he was away." At this Mia snorted laughter, and the judge asked her: "Is there something you wish to add, Miss McGregor?"

Mia laughed shortly. "Dad was not just 'not pleased,' he was fumin'. He nearly killed Sam, even though Sam had only done what mum asked, and had rescued me. It wasn't his fault mum went missin'. But dad's not one for logic…" she trailed off, and the judge wrote something on his papers, before gesturing for Mrs Kennedy to go on.

The lawyer had finished with Mia, however, and said so. The other lawyer, Miss Thornton, then got up and stood in front of the teenager.

"Miss McGregor," she said, "would you agree that Mr Harding put your life and your mother's life in danger by allowing you to DART to another universe?"

Mia sort of squinted at her, and raised one eyebrow. "Well, it wasn't *his* idea, it was mum's. She blackmailed him, didn't she?"

Now it was Miss Thornton's turn to blink. "Sorry?" she said.

Mia half-smiled. "Well, mum said she wouldn't give 'im 'is DARTs back unless he helped us escape to another reality. She made him do it."

Miss Thornton coughed. "Well," she said, "you cannot deny that Mr Harding's actions put you in danger and, indeed, may well have cost your mother her life. The fact he went against I-ART rules and allowed unregistered persons to use his DARTs resulted in your mother being missing, presumed dead."

Mia sniffed. "She's not dead until it's confirmed she is, thank you very much. And Sam only did what he had to. His bravery saved my life. Once I'd been kidnapped he could've left mum to it and got away. He'd done what she asked him to. He risked his life in order to save mine."

I smiled at her words. She was certainly good in an argument.

Miss Thornton gave up, said she was finished with the witness, and sat down. An agent led Mia back to her seat, and I nearly applauded.

The judge shuffled his papers, and had a word with an official, who then announced that it was time for a break. "We will reconvene in ten minutes' time," she shouted, and the judge went out through his back door.

Some of the crowd stood up and left the room, while others just chatted among themselves. I turned to Jake, who was sitting looking stunned. "Wow," he said.

I smiled. "Wow indeed, Jakey boy."

I asked the agent sitting next to us if we could leave the room, but they said we were to stay here. So Jake and I talked quietly until the ten minutes was up and the judge came back.

Once we had all sat down again, he spoke: "We

will not be hearing any more witnesses for the defence," he said, and I felt a surge of relief. That meant neither Jake nor I would have to go up there and be questioned.

He was continuing: "We will now hear from a representative of I-ART, the agency which Samuel Harding was working for when he absconded from duty, and from whom he stole the DARTs. Miss Thornton?"

The prosecution lawyer got up as an official called out: "Call James Waters."

A tall, skinny middle-aged man with a big bushy beard and a neat grey suit and black tie, Mr Waters stood straight as Miss Thornton approached.

As before, the judge said: "Can you please state your name for the court."

"James Waters," said the man. His voice was clear, but higher than I expected.

"And your occupation?" said the judge.

"Controlling Officer for the Practical Research Agency branch of I-ART, m'lud."

Miss Thornton stepped closer. “Mr Waters,” she said, “could you tell us how you know Samuel Harding?”

The man glanced at Sam, who was still standing in the same position as he had done throughout the trial. “Sam is – sorry, was – an agent under my command, Miss. I was his Controlling Officer, so he reported directly to me.”

“And can you tell us how many times Mr Harding disobeyed orders or went against the rules during the years under your command?”

Mr Waters smirked. “Well, Sam didn’t like being told what to do, Miss,” he said. “So I suppose he always did what he felt was best, not what we told him to do.”

“And did this flagrant disregard for authority ever lead to any problems?” asked the lawyer.

“Er… usually only for Sam, Miss,” said the man. “He got himself into all kinds of scrapes, but it was only ever because he was trying to help other people, not because he was trying to gain anything for himself."

This was obviously not going the way Miss Thornton wanted it to. In a rather strained voice, she went on: "Can you tell us what Mr Harding did on the day he was supposed to be handing in his DARTs and leaving the agency due to being made redundant?"

"Well, he didn't turn up at the agency when he was supposed to. He just disappeared, taking the DARTs with him."

"And can you tell us how much each of these DARTs cost?"

The man looked a bit bemused for a moment. "Er, well, they cost millions to develop," I saw Miss Thornton smile, but the smile soon disappeared, as Mr Waters went on: "but by the time the department was made redundant they were old technology, Miss. They're pretty useless now, given the new tech we now have."

The lawyer seemed to deflate. I don't think she had any arguments left. With a wave of her hand she mumbled "I have no further questions," and sat down.

I glanced at Sam, and I swear that, although he still looked drained and worried, there was a faint smile on his lips. His piercing blue eyes were bright.

The judge gestured to the two lawyers to go and speak to him, and they climbed the steps. They huddled together for two minutes, and the waiting crowd started to get restless. Mumbling was heard.

Then the judge shooed the lawyers away, coughed a few times, and I held my breath.

"I will now deliver my verdict," he called out loudly, making me jump.

This was it. I could barely breathe.

"Samuel Harding," he said, turning to address Sam. "You have pleaded guilty to the two charges put to you.

"We have heard from various sources that you are a principled, honest and well-meaning person who, nevertheless, cannot be trusted to follow rules even when they are meant to keep you safe.

"The character witnesses have proved that you are

a kind, generous and brave man who will risk his life to save those around him, not just his friends.

"In accordance, and after considering all the evidence put to me, the first charge, that of absconding from duty as an I-ART agent, we dismiss, due to you absconding on the last day of employment. You will face no punishment for that charge.

"For the second charge, that of stealing two DARTs, we sentence you to be banished from this reality and returned to the universe in which you have, for the last few months, made a life. The DARTs will not be returned to you, and you will have no way or returning to your own reality. I hope you live out the rest of your life in happiness and, hopefully, stay out of trouble. I wish you luck.

"Do you have anything to say?"

Sam looked puzzled by the whole thing, but suddenly he seemed to brighten, as I suppose he realised what the judge meant – he was going home with us! "No, my lord – I mean, thank you, my lord," he stammered.

I breathed a huge sigh of relief, someone in the audience clapped, and I heard Jake at the side of me shout out "yes!" as he, too, realised what it meant.

After all this adventure, after all the running, and the imprisonment, and the tension, and the worry, Sam was free.

And – even better – we were all going home.

Going home

That night was the best one we had had in a long time.

Once we'd been taken back to I-ART HQ, Jake and I were allowed to spend the rest of the day with Sam, mum and Lizzie. The agents even brought us some special food and drink, and we had a little party in the large meeting room, watching TV, playing games and eating cake until we felt sick.

One of the first things I did, after hugging Sam so tightly I thought he may break a rib, was to ask mum why she and Lizzie hadn't been at the trial.

"Lizzie was too upset, love," she explained, taking me to one side so my sister wouldn't hear. "She wouldn't stop crying, and I couldn't leave her alone for who knows how long, could I? Anyway, I was upset myself; I didn't know if I would be able to watch the trial without shouting at someone."

I laughed. I knew mum could never keep quiet whenever something upsetting was happening. I could well have imagined her leaping up mid-evidence and shouting “rubbish!” or “objection!”

Anyway, it was all going to be OK now, I thought, as I watched Sam jiggle Lizzie on his knee to make her laugh.

The agents said we would be taken home the next day, once all the formalities had been arranged – two agents would escort us back to our own reality, where we could settle back into our own blissfully normal routine. I was even looking forward to going back to school. Well, sort of…

There was, however, one thing everyone seemed to have forgotten about in the excitement.

It was Jake, of course, who brought it up. We were sitting, full of food, watching a quiz programme on TV, when he suddenly sat up straight, cake crumbs spilling out of his mouth. “What am I going to tell my mum and dad?” he shouted.

Everyone turned to look at him, and even Lizzie looked shocked.

Blimey. I hadn’t thought of that for a while. What

on earth could he say when he went home? His parents had no idea where he'd been these last, what? Three weeks or so?

Sam suddenly looked worried again. He opened his mouth as if to say something, then closed it.

Mum started to say that they would understand, then trailed off in mid-sentence. Of course they wouldn't understand. Their son had gone missing along with his best friend and best friend's family. There would have been no trace of us at all in our universe for weeks. The police, no doubt, would have been looking for us. For all we knew we might have made the evening news. I could imagine the headlines: Family disappear along with 11-year-old boy in their care.

How could we just pop back and say "It's OK, we're back now" without any explanation? I looked at Sam. He swore softly, then got up and went out. The doors were unlocked now that we were no longer prisoners, although I knew we weren't allowed to go outside.

He came back some time later, and we all looked at him expectantly.

"Well?" said mum.

Sam smiled. "They seem to think it'll be OK," he said, "though I'm not sure how. They're being a bit vague. Anyway, we mustn't let it spoil our evening. We're going home tomorrow, your parents will be fine again, Jake – I'll make sure they are."

Jake didn't look convinced, and I wasn't too sure either, but there was little we could do about it; and it was indeed nice to think we would all be home again the next day.

We went to bed late, tired but too excited to sleep much, and woke early, thrilled at the prospect of DARTing home. Jake couldn't keep still he was that excited, although he kept saying he didn't know what he was going to tell his mum.

After a hurried breakfast we packed our few belongings in bags provided for us (remember Jake and I had left our rucksacks in Dinoworld), and we were all bundled into a small room. I recognised it as the place Jake and I had returned to with agent Johnny after our adventure.

There were three agents there. One handed a sheet of paper to Sam, which he was asked to read and sign, while the others fussed about getting us into position.

Sam, Jake and I were to go with one agent, while mum and Lizzie went with the other. Mum was worried about something going wrong – especially after hearing, from Jake and I, what had happened to Mia's mum – but Sam reassured her: "The technology's so much better now, love," he said. "Even if you went to the wrong universe, which is now very unlikely, it could easily be fixed. We're not going to lose each other, I promise you."

And he kissed her and Lizzie before grabbing on to the agent's sleeve. Jake and I got hold of the other arm, bags at our sides. Altogether we made a rather crowded group, but we knew it wouldn't be for long – although it would take us three hours to get back home, it would merely seem like the blink of an eye.

As the agent pressed the DART button, I heard

Jake shout, as was now his habit, "Geronimo!"

....

I opened my eyes, and the light was bright. It was sunny. I could hear birds tweeting, and the distant sound of a car.

"There you go; all home again," said the agent, whose name was Tim.

I let go of his arm and looked around. Well, we were nearly home, at any rate – we were, in fact, at the bottom of our road. Sam was rubbing his eyes, Jake was jumping up and down in excitement, while, to our left, mum and Lizzie were hugging each other, while 'their' agent, Lucy, smiled at them.

"Wow," said Sam, as he realised where we were. "That technology really *has* improved. How do you programme it so close to where you want to be?"

Tim shook his head, and put his DART in the top pocket of his uniform jacket. "I'm not allowed to tell you that, sorry – orders are to keep you in the dark about the new stuff." He was laughing as he said it, and Sam laughed too.

"Come on, mum, let's go home!" That was Lizzie, shrieking at the top of her voice and dragging mum by the hand up the road, towards our house.

We started walking, and as we did Sam talked quietly to Tim.

As we turned into our driveway and walked up the path, it all felt unreal. The last time we had been here was the night Sam's alarm had gone off and he'd hurried us out of the house in the middle of the night.

It felt like we had been running ever since.

As mum put the key in the lock and turned it, I felt a huge sense of relief. We could stop now.

Inside, the house was dim and smelt musty. There were a few cobwebs in the hall, but within half an hour mum had opened all the windows to let the fresh air in, cold though it was, thrown away the rotten food from the cupboards (there was a half-eaten loaf of bread in there which I swear had several new lifeforms growing on it), removed the worst of the dust and, of course, had made everyone a cup of tea.

We all sat in the kitchen, mugs in our hands (mum even found an unopened, still in-date packet of biscuits to open), grinning from ear to ear.

Suddenly mum got up and went over to the calendar hanging on the notice board. "I don't even know what day it is!" she exclaimed. "Is it March yet?"

One of the agents told her it was now Tuesday, March 14th, so she turned the calendar over to the correct month and sat down again.

Jake was very quiet, I noticed. He was sipping his tea like it was alcohol.

After they'd finished their drinks the agents stood up, nodded to Sam, then said they needed to take Jake home now. My friend looked terrified. "It's OK, son," said Lucy, softly, "we're not DARTing again. You live not far away, yes?" Jake nodded. "Well, we said we'd get you home safely, so that's what we're doing."

We said our goodbyes on the doorstep, mum kissing Jake, Lizzie hugging him, and me asking him to let us know how it went as soon as he could.

Three hours later I was beginning to get really worried that the police may knock on the door at any time, asking us to "go to the station to help with their enquiries." But instead the phone rang, and Sam answered it.

I tried listening in, but all he seemed to be saying was "Yes, that's right."

The phone call lasted half an hour, and I was getting frantic with worry. Do the police arrest you over the phone now? I thought.

Finally, Sam put the phone down and turned to us. He looked strained, but he was grinning.

Mum was at my side. She had been trying to listen in, too. "What?" she asked. "Don't keep us hanging. Who was it?"

Sam ushered us into the living room, where Lizzie was playing with her dolls ("I missed you guys," she was telling them). We all sat down.

"It was Nigel, Jake's dad," began Sam. "He said Jake had returned home with two people, dressed in weird uniforms, who had told them that we and Jake had been on an adventure in another, parallel universe, but that everything had worked out fine and that they were bringing him home unharmed. They wouldn't answer any of his questions, saying it was classified information and that people's lives would be in danger if they so much as breathed a word of what they said to anyone other than our family.

"Jake's mum and dad didn't believe a word of it, of course – right until the moment the two people said goodbye, waved cheerily, pressed a button on a 'pebble' in their hands, and disappeared into thin air." I laughed, imagining the look on Sam's mum and dad's faces.

Sam went on: "Apparently they just sat there for ages, staring into the space where two people had just been standing, before asking Jake all sorts of questions. The poor boy must be exhausted by now.

"Anyway, eventually Nigel decided to ring me, to see if what the two people had said was true. Of course, I can't deny any of it."

"But what if they go to the police?" I asked. I was still worried Sam might end up in prison after all, this time for abduction or kidnapping or something.

"Well," said Sam, "the police have been looking for us since we left. We are officially missing persons. But Nigel is now going to ring them and say we have returned, that it was all a misunderstanding on his part, and that they can call off the search. They might ask some awkward questions, but I know Nigel's a resourceful man; he'll get round them somehow."

Mum breathed a heavy sigh of relief. "Thank God," she said. "We can all go back to normal." We all agreed that would be nice.

And it was, for a while at least…

A visitor

We didn't go back to school until the following week. It was good to be able to relax back into normality, bit by bit.

Mum phoned our schools and told them some complicated story about how we'd been called away during half-term to a dying relative in the middle of rural Scotland; how there was no landline or mobile phone reception there, so we couldn't get in touch; and how Jake's mum and dad had 'got the wrong end of the stick' about where he was.

I didn't expect anyone believed it; but Jake's mum and dad told the same story (what else *could* they say?) so the schools had to accept it. They threatened to fine mum for our 'unauthorised absence,' but I don't think she cared much either way.

Jake wasn't allowed to come to visit (I wasn't sure his mum and dad would *ever* let him out of the house again), but he managed to ring me a few times. He said his mum and dad were still in shock, that they kept asking him questions, some of which he didn't know how to answer, and that his mum and sister kept hugging him, but overall it was good to be home.

Neither he nor I had mobile phones anymore – they'd been left back in Dinoworld – so we both had to go shopping for new ones, which was nice. Sam bought me the latest model; I think he felt guilty about all we had been through. Lizzie complained, but was told she was too young to need one. Sam bought her a load of new toys instead.

Going back to school was hard. Everyone was asking us where we'd been, and we kept having to explain (well, tell lies). It was all very tiring.

But eventually the people in school stopped looking at us weirdly, Jake's mum and dad calmed down a little – although they refused to let Jake hang around with me or come to our house for a long time afterwards – and life returned to its normal, often boring routine.

It was nice.

Until…

It was the following summer. July. Jake and I were in the last couple of weeks of our first year in senior school. Jake had already had his twelfth birthday; I was nearing mine. Lizzie was now nine.

Sam had been promoted to head ranger, while mum had decided she was going to write a book based on our experiences. She'd always loved writing, and would spend hours huddled over the keyboard. Sam warned her she'd have to make it fiction, if she didn't want 'the men in white coats' to come and get her.

Jake and I were still best friends, although his mum and dad were very frosty towards us and had only just started letting him go out again. Sam had gone round there a few times to talk to them, and they had softened a little. I still think they didn't entirely believe the explanation for our disappearance, but they had no other.

And then, that Saturday in July, there was a knock at the door. Mum and Sam were out; I had been babysitting Lizzie, who was in her bedroom playing.

The girl at the door had changed her hair slightly – there were now bright pink streaks mixed in with the blue ones – but she was still wearing heavy black eyeliner and false eyelashes. She was wearing tight blue jeans, a white crop top and black slip-on shoes, and was carrying a rucksack which looked heavy. She put it on the ground as I answered the door.

"Hello Ethan," she said, brightly.

"Wha'?" I stuttered. "Mia?"

"That's me," she said. "Can I come in?"

Without really waiting for an answer, she pushed her way into the house, put her rucksack in the hall and headed to the kitchen.

"I could really do with a drink," she said. "I'm *parched*. I've been DARTin' around for hours tryin' to find you. Is Sam in?"

I followed her into the kitchen, where she was already looking in the fridge. She took out a can of Coke. "Alright if I have this?" I nodded, stunned. She sat down, opened the can and took a huge gulp.

"That's better," she said, before letting out a loud

burp. “Oops, pardon!”

I was looking at her as if she was an alien, which to all intents she was – I mean, she came from another universe, didn’t she? What was she doing here?

She took another long drink then put the can on the table. “I s’pose you want to know what I’m doin’ here,” she said. Well, that much was obvious, I thought.

“Er… yeah,” was all I could manage.

Mia reached into her front jeans pocket, pulled out a DART, and held it up in front of her face. What she said next made my stomach plunge down to my knees.

“I know how to find my mum, Ethan,” she said. “And I want you to help me rescue her.”

THE END

Pam Bloom was born in Liverpool, England, and now lives in nearby Meols, Wirral, with her husband, teenage daughter, cat and many, many fish. This is her second novel. She hopes you enjoyed it – if you did, she would love you forever if you gave her a review, however short, on the Amazon website.

The third book in the Parallel Universe Adventures trilogy will be published as soon as she can get round to finishing it.

For more details go to Pam's website, www.pambloomauthor, where you can sign up to her email list, or look her up on Twitter @PambloomPam, Goodreads, Google+ or facebook. She will be pleased to connect with you.

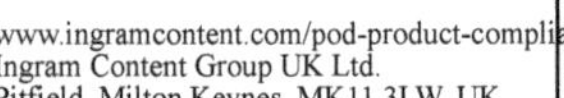
www.ingramcontent.com/pod-product-compliance
Ingram Content Group UK Ltd.
Pitfield, Milton Keynes, MK11 3LW, UK
UKHW020223250726
13967UKWH00001B/152

9 780995 527232